EDWIN BRIGHTWATER

A Vote For Death: A Novella

First published by Niels Jensen 2021

This novel is entirely a work of fiction. The names, characters and incidents portrayed in it are the work of the author's imagination. Any resemblance to actual persons, living or dead, events or localities is entirely coincidental.

Edwin Brightwater asserts the moral right to be identified as the author of this work.

Edwin Brightwater has no responsibility for the persistence or accuracy of URLs for external or third-party Internet Websites referred to in this publication and does not guarantee that any content on such Websites is, or will remain, accurate or appropriate.

Designations used by companies to distinguish their products are often claimed as trademarks. All brand names and product names used in this book and on its cover are trade names, service marks, trademarks and registered trademarks of their respective owners. The publishers and the book are not associated with any product or vendor mentioned in this book. None of the companies referenced within the book have endorsed the book.

First edition

ISBN: 978-957-43-9565-1

This book was professionally typeset on Reedsy.
Find out more at reedsy.com

In memory of how we used to be

Contents

1

Broken Glass

The screaming sounds of destroyed glass—cracking, bursting, shattering, smashing—charged the girl's ears roughly, without warning, in two tight bursts. The first burst came very loud, its destruction done with screeching, high-pitched brutality. The second shrieked lower down, more distantly, and for this seemed all the deadlier. It had a snap and crunch that made her think of something priceless being ground to dust.

In fright she leaped from bed and, wearing only pajamas, ran directly from her room to the landing at the top of the staircase. That evening her parents had sent her to bed much earlier than usual. The sun still hadn't properly gone down, though, and sleep was impossible. What she'd heard, the loud crash of shattering glass, had been, she was sure, no dream.

The girl stared down the flight of wooden stairs. The pale door that connected the base of the stairwell to the kitchen and dining room was shut tight. Through the door and up the stairs to her place on the landing, she could hear her parents slinging back and forth angry sentences. This scared her more. Ordinarily, they never argued.

She turned from the staircase and, as though this were her only option, went to the other bedroom on the upper floor of her two-story house. That was where Anna lived. The girl tip-toed inside and eyed Anna cautiously. The old lady was already in bed, eyelids clammed shut, snoring softly, though the bedside lamp hadn't been turned off and the old lady's library book lay open uselessly in her lap.

"Anna?" pleaded the girl. "Anna? Something's wrong. Are you awake?"

Slowly Anna opened her eyes and, after removing her glasses and using both palms to rub her sun-kissed face, looked back at the girl. "Mmm," said Anna. "It's all fine. Everything's fine. What's bothering you, dear girl?"

"There was a huge sound. Really loud. Like all the windows in the house breaking at once."

"That's peculiar. I didn't hear anything. Mind you, Mei-lin, my hearing's not what it used to be."

"You were asleep, Anna. That's why you didn't hear it."

Anna nodded thoughtfully, then asked, "Did your parents hear it?"

"I don't know. They're downstairs. That's where the sound came from. They're fighting."

"Oh my," said Anna, raising her eyebrows. "I … well … uh, you tell me, what day is it? Today?"

The girl, Mei-lin, told her. It was Sunday.

"Well, that's it, then. The government, they've announced their decision. I thought they'd do it later in the week, but the scoundrels"—she pronounced this word with gusto—"have got in early. Nothing we can do about it." She shook her head. "We'll get through it. Don't worry, my dear." And Anna smiled gently.

Mei-lin wondered whether Anna really understood all that was happening. Still, the old lady's answer left the girl feeling rather less concerned. That was better than nothing.

"Right," said Mei-lin. "So the decision that was made by the government, by the prime minister, it's about the, uh, the—it's about the referendum?"

Before Anna could answer, Mei-lin heard the door downstairs, the one that connected to the first story's kitchen and dining room, wrench open. Her father's voice boomed up the stairs.

"Mei-lin!" he cried. "Get your things. We're leaving. Anna, you too. We need to get out before they close the roads. Your mother will help you. I'll get the car ready." Then the girl heard her father stomping across to the house's attached garage.

Mei-lin's mother jogged up the stairs. With customary efficiency, not giving Mei-lin or Anna a single moment to ask questions, darting from one bedroom to the other, she organized their things in several small bags. Anna's pills, Mei-lin's documents (especially the adoption papers), warm clothes, plenty of socks, a couple of Anna's old photos, a book for Mei-lin: all these necessaries were packed away to join them on their escape.

Mei-lin offered up a composition book she used at school, explaining that she could use it for extra homework while they were away. Her mother rebuffed this. "You're only nine years old," she explained. "You don't need to do homework. Leave that behind."

Using her foot, Anna tapped the large and circular plastic container under her bed. "Fran, should we take this?" she asked Mei-lin's mother.

Fran, the mother, shook her head. "Nope. Not at all. You

don't use it anyway. And once we're out of here, we won't need it for … well, what they're going to do."

"But what are they going to do, Mum?" said Mei-lin, her eyes big and fearful.

"Don't let's talk about that right now, OK?" answered Fran. "We need to get going."

And so the girl, her mother, and the old lady went downstairs and, after collecting a few extra items from the large bedroom used by Mei-lin's parents, clambered into the car. Mei-lin's dad was already restlessly installed behind the wheel. The female passengers clutched tightly onto their handful of bags. Anna's circular chamber pot stayed behind, a dead mass of polymer under the elderly woman's bed.

* * *

As the family car pulled out into their small street and heaved toward the main road that ran out of town, Mei-lin could see that, though one or two other families seemed to have the same idea of escape, most were staying put. A couple of cars were parked out in their driveways, trunk and doors open, moms and dads and children filling them with essentials and then themselves piling inside. But everywhere else, their street looked as it would on any other middling summer evening in this tiny town in the heart of nowhere. Curtains drawn shut, gates and doors closed up, bedroom lights flicked on, each household's other lights steadily shutting down. As usual, Mei-lin thought to herself, her family chose to be different.

"Mum," said Mei-lin, "what was that sound? You know, the crashing sound? Just before we left home."

"Your father decided," said Mei-lin's mother dryly, "that not only could we afford a new television, but that we have so much money we can also pay to have the window in the living room replaced. At least we know that we don't need to fork out for bodybuilding training for your father, because he's so strong he can lift up a TV and throw it clean through the window without breaking a sweat."

Mei-lin's father knew when to fold. "Sorry, hon," he said meekly. "I'll make it up to you." He lowered his head and gripped the wheel tight, his eyes narrowing to focus on the darkening road.

"That you will, Frederick. That you will." Fran only addressed Mei-lin's father by this unabridged version of his name when she was very cross with him. Otherwise he was known—to his wife and everyone else—simply as Fred. "I think I'm owed a dishwasher for all of this," she added. "The kitchen's got space for one. We all know that."

Something about her mother's tone told Mei-lin that Fran's wifely grievances were not confined to the broken TV and smashed window. Though the girl grew increasingly curious, Mei-lin felt she'd best wait a moment or so before pestering her parents with more questions.

The car had left the township and was going north, traveling past dusky fields and murky rows of windbreak trees, wheels burring as they grabbed at the smooth road, its bitumen surface soon to climb the ranging foothills and cut through the mountain pass and plunge down into the next district and so separate the four travelers from their ill-treated and luckless home. No matter where Mei-lin might look, in every direction through the downward-drifting darkness she could see only black outlines of the mountain flanks circling her hometown. On all sides, they surrounded her and her family; from everywhere, they pressed down; no matter where she might try to go, she felt that true escape was impossible—thwarted everywhere by those faceless monsters sloping toward them through night's dark.

It was true that—for now, at least—there would be no escape. The little car crested a hill and, just as Fred was about to speed into the next stretch of night-time road, he hurriedly jammed the brakes. A web of blinking lights loomed there. The lights weaved and spun across the road and spread into the empty fields on each side. The brightest were up high, portable floodlights with thickly white beams that hurt Mei-lin's eyes. Others shone urgently from the headlamps of several parked vehicles.

These were mostly military. Mei-lin counted two jeeps, five or six canvas-clad trucks, and a bus full of soldiers who seemed to be waiting for orders. There was another vehicle, heavy and ominous-looking, that had a tank-like shell and huge black tires. Near the jeeps, Mei-lin spotted some civilian cars.

"What the …?" said Fred, meeting the gaze of a soldier with a rifle slung over his shoulder, who, standing in the middle of the road, frantically directed the car to pull over. "These aren't cops. They're army. And I don't reckon they're our army. The uniforms look different."

As soon as her father had turned off the road, soldiers surrounded the car. An older man in a peaked cap leaned through Fran's window and waved around a flashlight, shining it carefully in each of their faces. Mei-lin's startlement beginning to subside, she wondered what the soldiers would make of the four of them. In the front sat her mother and father, both blond and pale-skinned, each a few years short of middle age. In the back, perched behind the driver's seat, was Anna, an old and dark-eyed woman with olive-colored skin and a jutting

Roman nose. She looked as if she belonged on the other side of the world—the coastal edges of the Levant, perhaps—and not here, in the rural backwaters of New Zealand's South Island.

And then there was the youngest member of the quartet, Mei-lin, who, sitting behind her mother, exhibited features indisputably East Asian: thick black hair; copperish skin (she was nicely tanned after a summer spent outdoors); and her nose and lower jaw small and well-defined. In their tiny town, there was no one else like Mei-lin. Her Asiatic appearance ruled out all possible genetic connection to the car's other occupants.

Giving no greeting or introduction, the soldier asked Mei-lin's father for their names and purpose of travel. He spoke with an odd accent that was part European, part North American. He sounded nothing like anyone local.

"I'm Fred Johnson," her father said in answer. "This is my wife, Fran. In the back is my daughter, Mei-lin. Also there in the back is Mrs. Anna Katz, who lives with us. She's a family friend. We're going on a drive to visit relatives."

"Travel outside the town is not permitted," said the soldier in his foreign accent. "Except with the written authority of your country's Minister for Internal Affairs, which I think you do not have."

"We won't be gone long," said Fred, somewhat sheepishly, as if he knew all too well that this kind of bland defense wouldn't right a sinking ship.

With a pained expression, the soldier ignored Fred's answer and looked over at Anna. "I assume the lady in the back is over seventy-five. Am I correct?"

Fred nodded.

"No, no, this cannot do." The soldier began to shake his head. "You must wait until the referendum is implemented. That is your government's order."

Leaning toward the soldier, trying to move things in a different direction, Fran quietly asked, "You're not from around here, are you?"

The soldier paid no attention to Fran's question. Turning his gaze to Mei-lin, he flicked his fingers at the girl and said, "She doesn't look like your daughter."

"I am their daughter," responded Mei-lin. "I'm adopted. I was born in Taiwan and came to New Zealand as a baby. Don't you know that some children are adopted?"

At her answer, both parents smiled; Fred began sniggering. Mother and father were so heartfully proud of Mei-lin, their clever, sassy daughter, and her retort to the rude foreigner was well said. But the girl's show of childish impudence seemed to embarrass and irritate the soldier. He tut-tutted. His face distorted darkly. Mei-lin suddenly felt she might have made a terrible mistake.

Anna came to their rescue. With no advance warning—none at all, not a wave of the hand, not a nod of the head—the old lady leaned forward, smiled brightly, and began talking at the soldier in rapid-fire French. Startled, he tipped his face back, as if he couldn't believe his own ears. In this South Pacific nation, they spoke only English and, in some areas and households, the old indigenous language. But the exotic-looking elderly lady kept talking at him in French.

After a moment or two, eyebrows lifting, eyes brightening, frown softening, the soldier responded in the same language. His initial replies, no more than a terse word or two, soon yielded to a merry, animated conversation in which both participants appeared to share life stories and become firmest of friends.

This went on for several minutes. Eventually, as if he truly wished to continue the conversation all night and only the insistent demands of military life forced him to withdraw, the soldier slapped the roof of the car with a kind of Gallic reluctance. Reverting to English, he exclaimed, "How marvelous! What an interesting lady you have here. But I am afraid I must insist. You must go home. My colleagues will drive with you. We must see that you have a safe journey."

Fred turned the car about and they drove back toward their little town. One of the civilian vehicles was dispatched to follow, steered carefully by a man in a pale suit. He had two soldiers for passengers. Just as their escort pulled out after them, Mei-lin's father twisted about in his seat and caught a glimpse of the car's license plates.

"Diplomatic plates!" spat Fred. "Those guys are with a foreign embassy. Must have driven all the way here from up north. I can't see which country they're from, though."

"Well," said Anna, "that young major was Canadian. He told me that he was from Montreal. Very charming he was, once I let him get going. If I had to put my money on it, though, I'd say he had a Quebec City accent. The fellow didn't seem too happy to be here. I'm not sure why, it's a lot colder over in Canada, the winters are truly awful."

Mei-lin's eyes lit up in amazement. "That's so cool, Anna! You can tell where someone comes from by how they speak French. You're like a spy!"

Anna chuckled. "If I am, I'm just about the world's oldest spy. I wouldn't be much use. You might as well cart me off to the glue factory."

This talk of spies sparked Mei-lin's abundant imagination. "Mum," she inquired, "do you think this has anything to do with the shuttle that blew up?" The girl was referring to the destruction of a United States space orbiter a few weeks earlier. The disaster was all over the news. Everyone on board—all five astronauts, including a lady teacher—had been killed when the orbiter's rockets and fuel tank exploded seconds after lift-off.

"No, Mei-lin. I can't see any connection," replied Fran. "We live in strange times. That's all."

One of Mei-lin's earliest memories of the wider world was from 1981, when she'd been four years old and someone shot and killed President Reagan. She remembered how scared and sad everyone was. Her father often complained that the world started going downhill the moment they got rid of Reagan.

"Remember, hon," Fred said, "last year, when Ferraro came out to visit?" He was referring to the incumbent vice president of the United States. "She was here a whole week. Everyone wondered why she was here so long. It wasn't like she was touring the country, it was just meetings up north. She's the most powerful woman in the world, hon. She doesn't have time to screw around. I reckon they were up to something. Something big."

Mei-lin was excited by the thought of a grand international conspiracy cooked up in her homeland, these tiny and trifling islands of New Zealand. Still, she thought her father's theory would prove too optimistic. His enthusiastic ideas about politics and current affairs usually saw themselves swiftly overturned by the next day's news.

"It could be, Fred. Anything's possible," said Fran. "What we know for sure is that there are foreign soldiers here in our own country ordering us around. My father would be turning in his grave."

Fred harrumphed, his foot sinking into the gas pedal, the car speeding into a long stretch of straight road. "Too true. That he would. It's a bloody disgrace, damn right."

Their escort followed them all the way home. The car with diplomatic plates parked opposite their driveway, the pale-suited driver and two soldiers peering out like flesh-and-blood gargoyles. Though very tired, Mei-lin took her time to get ready for bed, unpacking her bags slowly, brushing her teeth and changing into pajamas more fastidiously than usual. Even so, when she peeked out her bedroom window just before crawling under the sheets, she saw that the car and its strange occupants were still there—still watching, still waiting, a posse of stalwart hunters slinking through the night.

2

French Lessons

The next morning the car had gone. At breakfast, Fran announced that Mei-lin would skip school that day.

"There's too much going on," said Fran. "I know you don't like to miss school, especially Mondays. But last night was really stressful. A quiet day at home with Anna will settle things down."

Though Mei-lin loved school, she loved Anna even more. The girl easily acquiesced. As soon as breakfast was over, her mother left for work. Fran would take just a few minutes to drive to the headquarters of the town government, where she efficiently helped with typing, filing, scheduling, and other administrative concerns. Mei-lin's father had already departed, embarking early on his motorbike for the auto repair business that he and a cousin ran together.

"Your father and I will try to come back during the day to check on you," her mother said as she went. "He says the workshop shouldn't be too busy. And I can get away from the office for a few minutes."

But during the day Mei-lin saw nothing of her parents.

Fortunately, she hardly noticed the absence. Thanks to Anna, the girl had a busy, cheery, carefree day, the kind so often enjoyed by those with happy memories of a happy childhood.

Mei-lin and the old lady started their morning in the garden, where Anna inspected flower beds and fruit trees and potted plants and instructed Mei-lin as necessary. "Pull out those weeds, my dear," she said. "That branch, Mei-lin, it could do with a bit of trimming. Can you reach that high?" she asked. "Yes, my dear, that's the way, a little bit more off and it's perfect," she said. Mei-lin treasured every second of this mutual effort. Teamed up with Anna, she was valued, listened to, affirmed. She was a real person in her own right. Like this, as the old lady's amanuensis, she could have gardened all day.

But the sun straggled higher and the heat of midday arrived. They went inside and ate a chat-filled lunch of ham sandwiches and buttery cookies. Anna took her post-prandial nap. As the old lady slept, Mei-lin sat cross-legged on her bedroom floor and, with quiet pleasure, swiftly consumed another of the books she'd borrowed from the middle-school section of the town library.

Anna woke up. As the old lady gulped down a fresh cup of strong tea, Mei-lin meticulously recounted the labyrinthine plot of her library book. Now rested and restored, the two partners-in-crime marched to the kitchen. The afternoon sprawled before them, and this demanded some serious baking.

They began with cheese scones. At these, Anna was a past master. One time, Fred had eaten six of Anna's scones in rapid succession, unable to resist each ripe, airy roundel of flour (the self-rising kind), butter (salted, of course), cheddar cheese, and farm-fresh whole milk.

Once the scones were baked golden and crispy and stood

to cool on the kitchen's fawn countertop, the old lady and young girl blended up a batch of cookie dough. The recipe was provided by Mei-lin, copied out by hand from an old cookbook she'd come across visiting a classmate's house the year before. The classmate's mother had used the recipe to sumptuous effect, unveiling from her oven sweet and crunchy and beautiful cookies—coarsely shaped, their flesh cocoa-darkened, each plainly seasoned with mighty helpings of broken peanuts.

Under Anna's guidance, Mei-lin had the same superb results with her own cookies. After taking the dark treats from the oven and waiting for them to cool off, Anna quaffing another mug of tea to pass the time, the two cooks boxed everything up and stowed the fruits of their labor in the kitchen larder. Mei-lin stacked away the last of the containers, each one evidence of an afternoon's well-spent domestic effort, and felt herself brim and swell with pride and belonging.

It was late in the afternoon, the long, low light of summer evening descending steadily, and the girl's parents had still not returned home. With time on their hands, Mei-lin retrieved the textbook that Anna used to instruct the girl in the French language. The book was dog-eared, scuffed and grubby, a remnant of the sparse decade that followed the Second World War. But it was precise and straightforward and in their earlier lessons Mei-lin had already made fine progress.

Of course, she had an outstanding exemplar of a teacher. When a child herself, Anna had learned the language from her parents. Then, in the years before the war, she had worked in Belgium and Switzerland. Though the old lady also spoke German, she had outright refused to teach Mei-lin a single word of that language. "Not after what they did during the war, my dear," Anna had told her. "Anyhow, it's a terribly ugly language.

Brings to mind a dog that can't make up its mind between barking and farting. I suppose it rather suits the Krauts, if you think about it." This was the crudest thing Mei-lin would ever hear Anna say.

That day they had been at their French lesson for at least an hour, Mei-lin growing hungrier and hungrier as the afternoon folded irretrievably into evening, Anna now looking tired and distracted, when they heard from the direction of the street outside the grunt and belch of her father's motorbike. He parked the machine in the garage, and Mei-lin thought she could hear the bike scrape against the steel frame of his workbench. It was an odd moment of carelessness in her father's handling of his prized motorcycle.

Fred strode inside. He marched to the living room, on the way barely acknowledging his daughter and the old lady where they sat at the dining table finishing up Mei-lin's French lesson. A musty tarpaulin, installed by Fred early that morning, covered the largest window in the living room. This was the window whose glass pane had been destroyed when Fred, wild with anger and frustrated as hell, had heaved up the family television set the night before and thrown it clean through the window.

"Yep, it'll do for the time being," said Fred, patting the tarpaulin, nodding down at his daughter, who now stood beside him in the living room. "Pretty stupid of me, huh? Your mother's furious about it. She'll want a new car on top of that dishwasher, I bet. It won't be long until you ladies run the world. About time, too. Us fellas haven't been doing too well in that department."

Fred went into the kitchen and, persisting in the face of spirited opposition from Anna, set about cooking their evening meal. "I phoned Fran before I left work and she said she doesn't know when she'll be home. Says it's crazy in the office," he told Anna. "So I can make us dinner." But all Fred knew in the kitchen was how to poach eggs. So for dinner the three of them ate sloppy eggs over burnt and butter-smeared toast.

By the time Fran got home from work, Anna had already tottered upstairs and retired for the evening. Fran appeared exhausted, as if she'd crammed a whole month of impossible work into a single fraught Monday. Gnawing through half a scone and one of Mei-lin's peanut-and-cocoa cookies, Fran slumped at the dining table and recounted to Fred and Mei-lin her woeful day.

"I don't see how it can be done. Compiling the lists, cross-checking the data, notifying eligible residents, organizing and setting up rooms for the function itself. All before Saturday! Not to mention the psychological aspect. We try not to think about what we're actually doing, but you can't suppress things forever. Of course, we're not supposed to talk about it, not in that way."

"I know, hon," said Fred. "Just keep your head down. We've already tried to get out of it. We've done all we can."

"But, Mum," asked Mei-lin, "what's going to happen on Saturday?"

Her parents exchanged uneasy glances across the table. There was a messy pause. Then Fran sighed and said, "There's going to be a banquet, Mei-lin. Everyone in town will have to go. We'll sit down together and eat, as if we're at a really big wedding. It's taken us by surprise. No-one was expecting it to happen. But at least it'll be over and done with in the next few days."

Mei-lin was confused. It sounded quite nice, this banquet, and she'd always enjoyed going to weddings. But if that was all it was, why had her world so swiftly become scary and strange?

She had to get to the bottom of things. She knew, though, that direct inquiry on delicate matters usually went nowhere with her parents.

"Oh," she said. "Um … is banquet a French word, Mum?"

"It could be," answered her mother. "Best to ask Anna in the morning. Don't worry, Mei-lin, you mightn't need to attend at all. It could just be your father and me. They're still deciding what to do about the children. Everyone under eighteen, of course, they can't vote yet."

"What about Anna, then? Will she go? Or will I stay home with her?"

Before her mother could respond, the phone rang loudly. Outside all was black, the hour well past Mei-lin's usual bedtime. The three of them jumped at the unexpected noise, as if suddenly fearful that fate had begun battering its way into their home.

Fran ran to answer. The telephone set was in the hall, and she shut the door behind her, and Mei-lin and her father heard just the odd sibilant consonant and much long silence.

By the time Fran had hung up the receiver and returned to the dining table, she was deathly pale. "That was a long-distance call, someone from the Bureau of Schools, phoning all the way from up north," she explained. "They said they'd been informed that Mei-lin wasn't at school today and wanted to know why. I was going to give them a piece of my mind, but then I realized that maybe we'll have to play along, at least until this is over. I've got my situation at work to think about."

Fred nodded silently. Mei-lin, gazing downward and away from everything, fumbled with the hem of her linen shorts.

"Tomorrow, Mei-lin, you'll have to go back to school," her mother said. "Keep your head down. None of your typical investigating or asking questions about this and that. We just need to get through until Saturday. We do that, and afterward it's all behind us."

They sent her to bed. As she trudged up to her room, the low hiss of her parents' whispers receding into nightful stillness, Mei-lin's stomach knotted fearfully. She felt that she could see the future before her, and it was a terrible thing: the whole world about to invert itself and become monstrous.

3

Crime

The girl slept badly. She grouched her way through breakfast. By the time she arrived at school, her mood was foul. Her spirits lifted, though, as she approached her homeroom, a familiar place of safe routine. She stowed her backpack, tucked her bare legs under the allotted desk, and, as the teacher took attendance, forced herself to observe, to think, to plan.

As soon as she'd paid full attention, Mei-lin saw that, though she'd only been away a single day, the classroom had changed. The pupils' desks were bunched together to make space at the rear for a new entrant: a pasty, stern-faced woman in her fifties who, like a peevish hawk, constantly watched them all. Her eyes were beady, and they seethed hardness. Her hair was jet-black and cut into a loose bob. It made Mei-lin think of a painted steel helmet.

A classmate whispered that the woman's name was Mrs. Gill. She came from up north and had been stationed in their classroom since yesterday morning. Others like her were spread across the school. No-one was very certain what Mrs. Gill's job was, but all of them—Mei-lin's classmates, the venerated teacher, even the school's craggy principal—were dead scared of her. She did little. She said little. Yet, from mere presence and bearing alone, she had them by the short hairs. They behaved as if she were a gargoyle who could roar to life and tear them to shreds for the least misdeed.

The teacher was very nervous, and the students very listless and ill at ease, and no-one learned much of anything before the bell rang and morning recess arrived. Mei-lin bolted outside, leaving in her backpack the fruity snack (this morning, a bruised banana) she'd usually munch heartily while playing with classmates. Instead, she corralled together two of her closest friends. They were a freckled girl and a brown-eyed boy. The trio often climbed an old oak tree that stood near the school's main gate. Mei-lin ran to the tree and, going ahead of her friends, scampered up toward the old oak's highest limbs. The other two joined her, though reluctantly, without their usual verve, as if they knew too well that no good would come of this.

"What's going on?" Mei-lin asked. "Everything's so weird."

"We're not supposed to talk about it," said the boy. "You weren't here yesterday. The teachers said we just have to act like normal. Mrs. Gill and the other ones like her, they've been sent down to make sure."

Mei-lin frowned. "But what's happening on Saturday? And how is that to do with the referendum? Don't you want to know?"

The freckled girl shook her head. "Mei-lin, we're really not supposed to talk about it. If Mrs. Gill finds out, it's not just us who get into trouble, our parents get into trouble too. My parents are having enough trouble already. My dad said that the slaughterhouse has been suddenly closed down. He had a whole lot of cattle, hundreds of them, that he was going to send there this week and now he can't. He says that's never happened before. He doesn't know what to do, he says that if the cattle can't go through the slaughterhouse, then they're no good to him or anyone else."

Now the brown-eyed boy frowned. "What? My cousin was living at the slaughterhouse. He stayed in one of those old houses they have for the workers. But now he's come to stay with us. It happened last night. He's still going to work, though. He says that it's even busier than usual, everyone is cleaning everything out, even the old houses they stay in. They're only got a few days to get it all done, he told me."

"Why's that?" asked Mei-lin. "What's going to happen at the slaughterhouse?"

"Hey, I don't know!" exclaimed the boy, his voice sharpening tetchily. "My mum's super stressed, she doesn't like my cousin. He drinks too much beer and makes a mess. There's not enough room for him in our house. I thought maybe he could go stay with my grandparents, their house is really big. But something's happened, suddenly we're not allowed to go and see them. Mum said it's because they're not feeling well. She looks really sad, though, as if she's never going to see them again or something. I just try not to think about it. She says we have to pretend that everything's normal."

Mei-lin bit her lower lip. None of this made sense. "The slaughterhouse is huge. There are so many people working there," she said. "Whatever's happening, it's pretty major."

"No kidding," said the brown-eyed boy. "Hey, Mei-lin, we heard about your family. How you tried to escape town. Mrs. Gill told us yesterday. She said that you're a bad example."

Mei-lin shrugged indifferently. "Doesn't really matter. There were so many soldiers, there was no way we could have got out," said Mei-lin. "It was like an old war movie."

"Look, really, I don't think we should talk about this," said the freckled girl. "We're not supposed to. Anyway, we're just kids, no-one tells us anything. My parents say it'll all be over by next week. Let's just wait until then."

An angry voice suddenly bawled at the three children. From their perch high in the oak tree, they looked down. Mrs. Gill was stomping back and forth, eyes blazing furiously, hands balled into fists, compelling the trio groundward.

"Get down! Now! Get out of that tree!" she screamed. "You horrible children!" She thumped the side of the tree with her open palm, as if it were the rump of a slow-minded cow that needed urging along toward the butcher's knife.

The freckled girl and brown-eyed boy scrambled to the ground. As they ran past Mrs. Gill, rushing to the relative safety of their homeroom, the woman hissed bitterly at the two children. Mei-lin slowly descended in their wake, taking her time, fussing over each foothold and handhold provided by the oak tree's broad trunk. She wanted to draw Mrs. Gill's attention to herself and away from her two friends. It was Mei-lin who'd instigated their secret conference in the treetops. She alone should bear responsibility, the girl told herself.

"Stupid girl!" spat Mrs. Gill. "I know what you were talking about up there. Don't think I don't know. How stupid!"

"I'm very sorry, Mrs. Gill," said Mei-lin. She made her voice tremble. She blinked heavily, trying to touch off a few tears of remorse. But her eyes were no help. They stayed decidedly dry. "Mrs. Gill, it's all my fault. I wasn't at school yesterday, I didn't realize—"

Mrs. Gill smacked Mei-lin's left ear hard, using her open-palmed hand as if it were a bat for crushing insects. Tears welled in the girl's eyes. Thank God, Mei-lin thought. At least I'm crying now.

"I'm sorry, Mrs. Gill. I really am."

"No, you're not. Don't lie to me, girl. You're trash. You and all your family."

Mei-lin's stomach roiled angrily. The unorthodox set-up of her family made her very sensitive to this kind of attack. She imagined punching Mrs. Gill in the face, knocking her over, smearing the woman's head with mud and sand gouged from the wet soil below. But Mei-lin knew she couldn't do this. These are special times, she told herself.

Lowering her head, Mei-lin turned from Mrs. Gill and ran like the wind back to her classroom. For the rest of the day's lessons, Mei-lin sat quiet as a mouse, only speaking to the teacher when asked, saying not a word to her classmates, and giving Mrs. Gill the coldest of cold shoulders.

She would not arrive home from school until very late, almost past the typical dinnertime. This happened because, for the first time since anyone could remember, all the students were kept on after the school day's scheduled lessons had finished, all required to attend a special assembly, then organized into large groups to tidy and clean and, when no more tidying or cleaning could be done, jog in slow loops around the school's playing fields.

Her parents were chatting in the dining room and didn't seem to hear Mei-lin come home. Sitting in the hall and tugging apart her shoelaces, she furtively eavesdropped on Fred and Fran's conversation.

"At least the question of the children is sorted out," said her mother. "They're expected to attend, but there's no requirement that they participate. We should be grateful for small mercies, I suppose."

Her father's reply to this was a short, vague mumble.

"I don't know how the over seventy-fives are taking it. I do think it's worst for them," Fran continued. "What a thing to go through at the end of a long life! Talk about going out with a bang."

Of her father's reply, Mei-lin could only make out a single word: "Anna."

"No, I haven't discussed it with her," responded Fran. "There's already that problem with her medication. We've done what we could. No point in crying over spilt milk."

Feeling bad about all this eavesdropping on her parents, Mei-lin put away her shoes and padded into the dining room. Fran and Fred looked at her in gladdened surprise.

"Home at last!" exclaimed her mother. "They told us that school would be running late today. For the rest of this week, as well. I'll get dinner going, I've had it warming in the oven. Can you tell Anna it's time to eat?"

As Anna shuffled out of her bedroom and down the stairs to the dining room, and while Mei-lin's mother readied things in the kitchen, Mei-lin tried to share with her father what she'd heard about the odd goings-on at the slaughterhouse. He nodded cautiously, his shoulders slouching forward and head drooping, as if he already knew but would do everything for none of it to be real.

"Best not to yak about this kind of thing, sweetheart. Don't want to make things difficult for your mother." Fred looked dolefully toward the kitchen, where Fran was dismembering a roasted chicken. Her mother hewed to New Zealand's rural tradition of overcooking every kind of meat. Mei-lin wished there'd be plenty of gravy, which was the single true cure she knew for fowl so stringy you could just about knit its skeins into mittens. "It's hard for her already," continued Fred. "In her office they're doing most of the organizing for Saturday."

As Mei-lin chewed through the evening meal, Fran relayed the highlights of her day. Most of it had been spent with officials from up north who'd been sent down to oversee the town's preparations for Saturday. Her mother described a new kind of meeting where co-workers were expected to point out failings in each other's performance. Although the thought of this made Mei-lin uneasy, she guessed that it wasn't the absolute worst of what her mother had to face. Fran's shoulders looked stiff, and she held her knife and fork at odd angles. She seemed pinched and listless. Probably lots of other things, all even more horrible, were happening at work. But to protect her daughter, Fran would have censored all that out.

The four of them were having dessert when the old lady remarked that her blue pills were just about run out. Her doctor had long been ordering her to take one of these blue pills with each morning's breakfast. Fran replied that she'd checked already on Anna's behalf at the drugstore, they didn't have any of her blue pills in stock, and on account of the general situation it was impossible for more to be delivered this week. The pharmacist had advised that anyone running short should try splitting the pills in two and taking half the usual dose. Anna would need to do this, said Fran. It'd see her out, she explained, get her through the last few days.

"I expect I'll cope," said Anna sunnily. "It's been a long life. I can get through a little bump in the road before the Grim Reaper comes along."

All night, as Mei-lin lay in bed tossing and turning, unable to sleep, the girl was consumed by an unrelenting mental image of the Grim Reaper. That cloaked, scythe-wielding figure was now among them, she imagined. And soon, well before the girl had any hope of being ready, he would come for them and claim his due.

4

Punishment

Mei-lin hardly slept that night. When she arrived at school, she was drowsy and didn't notice the principal stumbling toward her, one hand raised as if flagging a New York taxi.

"Mei-lin Johnson! Mei-lin!" he croaked. She had just crossed a gravelly basketball court, her homeroom a few paces away. The bell that signaled the school day's beginning would ring any minute. "You're not going to your homeroom today, young lady. They want to keep an eye on you. Come with me."

The principal led her to the opposite end of the campus, where the oldest students were taught for two or three years before being freed into adulthood. As they walked, Mei-lin had a clear view of the varicose veins that burrowed like bruised worms across the old man's calves. She hoped she'd never marry someone whose legs might ever look like that.

The principal made the girl sit at the back of a classroom belonging to a teacher of calculus, trigonometry, statistics, and connected oddities. He handed her a dense wad of worksheets and told her to complete them. "If you finish all of those, then start on these books," said the principal, piling up several volumes from the school library that she realized instantly she'd already read during the summer break.

The principal left. The room quickly filled with senior high school students. The teacher began chalking an equation on the board. Just as the math teacher cleared his throat to address the class, Mrs. Gill marched in. Ignoring the teacher, she strode to the back of the room and drew up a chair near Mei-lin.

"From now on, girl, you'll do exactly what you're told," rasped Mrs. Gill. "We won't stand for any nonsense. If I had my way, you'd get a thorough thrashing. Perhaps I'll still be able to get my way. If you don't like the sound of that, shut your mouth and behave, you silly little girl."

Mei-lin gulped and stared down at the worksheets and strained to collect herself. She rubbed her jaw. She tugged her ear. She kneaded her temples. She thought about how old Mrs. Gill was and how the nasty woman would be dead much sooner than Mei-lin. Her anger and fear began to subside. She began to feel herself again.

For the rest of the morning, her emotions were held in firm check. Mei-lin religiously ignored Mrs. Gill. She also avoided speaking to anyone else, whether the eighteen-year-olds battling mathematical peculiarities in this classroom or her own friends in the playground when she was allowed outside at recess.

By lunchtime, her bout of quiet, focused effort meant she'd completed the worksheets. But when she started on the pile of books the principal had given her, Mei-lin found herself resisting this new task. It was tiresome and enervating. What's the joy in reading a story you've already read before? A story without surprises, without tension, without unanswered questions?

Her mind wandered. Cautiously, without looking up from her desk, not wanting Mrs. Gill to accuse her of daydreaming or some other crime, Mei-lin began to think everything through. The situation was awful: the news on Sunday night, which had been so bad that her father threw the TV through a window; their attempt to escape, thwarted by the foreign soldiers and the roadblock; all the strange preparations for Saturday's banquet, which had some some kind of connection to a mysterious referendum and also involved the closing of the slaughterhouse. Then you had Mrs. Gill and the other outsiders in Mei-lin's school, monitoring everyone, ruthlessly keeping all of them in line; everyone everywhere so busy, so tense, though never speaking of what really was happening.

Mei-lin remembered Anna telling her about Hitler and all the evil things he'd done, like starting the war and putting the Jews into camps and gassing them to death. What struck the girl was that, according to Anna, no-one in the early days really knew that Hitler's government would become so awful. When he came to power, their world did change. Life in Germany became stranger and stranger, some things got better, many things got worse. But this all happened in small steps. Like frogs in a cauldron of plain water slowly being taken to the boil, most people didn't realize that they were on their way to death and destruction. That, Anna thought, was why so few people tried to stop Hitler before it was too late.

And that wasn't all. Anna explained that, shortly after the war, she'd visited one of the camps where the Nazis killed the Jews. It was the saddest place she'd ever seen. Even the birds in the trees refused to sing. But today, Anna told Mei-lin, all these decades later, there are still people in Germany, and in other places, who can't bring themselves to talk about these terrible things. Some won't even admit that Hitler's death camps existed at all. These people turn their heads and act like nothing ever happened.

Mei-lin challenged Anna on this. No sensible person could be so ignorant, especially since the Second World War was over a long time ago and the facts were so clear. "My dear," replied Anna, "you'd be amazed the things that people do when they want to get rid of bad feelings, of anything that makes them feel uncomfortable. They're quite capable of letting their hearts stretch until they snap right in half."

Mei-lin strove to draw together the strands she saw before her. Something bad was happening here in her hometown. She worried that, though it started small, just tiny flecks of darkness here and there, in the end the light would all go and evil would engulf them all. It involved the referendum, the government, the slaughterhouse, old people, a banquet happening on Saturday. It was so awful that none of the adults could speak of it. It was so awful that now, very close to its happening, the true shape of its horror still lay largely beyond her perception.

The girl's nine-year-old mind tumbled about wildly, proffering and dispatching and revisiting and discarding once more a series of mad theories. Her mind ranged as far and wide as young imagination would allow, swooping from the sublime to the grotesque and up and over again. One idea in particular nagged her. She found herself returning to it over and over. The idea was horrible, its enactment seemed impossible, but it had a powerful logic that seemingly tied together all that she knew. And of all her ideas, this alone truly accounted for the slaughterhouse.

But ... no! They surely wouldn't do that, would they?

Clearing out the slaughterhouse, scrubbing it down, making the equipment ready for new uses: there must be some alternate reason. Then again, Mei-lin thought, that's probably what the Germans said when all the Jews living among them in their towns and cities were led away. They would never have imagined that those friends and neighbors and colleagues and classmates were soon to be slaughtered like so many stunned, insensible sheep.

The teacher finished the day's last math lesson. Mrs. Gill rapped her knuckles against Mei-lin's desk, wagged a bony finger at the girl, its tip almost catching Mei-lin's nose, and then wordlessly strutted from the classroom. As soon as Mrs. Gill had vanished from view, Mei-lin and the senior students were ordered outside. Instead of being dismissed and sent home, as they had all expected, the teacher cajoled the reluctant students into a series of interminably dull ball games. He seemed to be acting under orders, as if he had no choice. Mei-lin was excused from active involvement on the grounds that she was too young and too small and too slow. Which she didn't mind one bit. As far as the girl could tell, the single, true purpose of the impromptu games was wasteful diversion of everyone's time.

So Mei-lin spent the rest of the afternoon sitting cross-legged on the ground, watching these pointless games and ruminating spectacularly. In her mind, the terrible theory she'd developed about the referendum and the slaughterhouse and Saturday's banquet continued to fester. Though she tried to quell these wild thoughts, it was in vain. And thus Mei-lin made a decision. As soon as she got home that evening, she'd confront her parents with her outrageous theory. She would demand answers.

It was late, almost dinnertime, before the teacher released

the senior students from their games and ordered everyone home. As she anxiously approached her house, Mei-lin noticed a strange silver van parked just outside. She'd never seen it before. She was certain that no-one in her street owned a van like that. Mei-lin recalled her mother's warnings about stranger danger and the bad people who kidnapped young children. Her pulse quickened, the hairs of her neck stood on end, and she sprinted the last few paces home.

But what Mei-lin saw as she rushed inside was even more horrifying. Sitting at the dining room table, facing both her parents, who wore resigned, listless expressions, was Mrs. Gill. Behind the spiteful woman's chair rested a small suitcase. In an instant, Mei-lin realized what had happened. Her family had been made prisoners in their own home. Mrs. Gill was now billeted with them—an unwelcome guest, an unwanted overseer.

Mrs. Gill turned and glared sourly at Mei-lin. Taking the initiative, Mei-lin asked as jauntily as she could, "Mrs. Gill, are you staying with us?"

"How observant of you, Mei-lin," said Mrs. Gill tartly.

"Glenys—I mean, Mrs. Gill—uh, yes, that's right, she'll be staying with us for the rest of the week," said Mei-lin's mother, trying to sound as if Glenys Gill were a distant cousin who'd made a sudden, unplanned but gladly received visit. "Until Saturday. There are so many people in town to help with organizing everything. They decided to board some of them with us locals. Mei-lin, I've arranged to put Mrs. Gill in your room. Anna says she doesn't mind if you bunk down in hers. When it's time for bed, I'll lay out your sleeping bag."

Her father nodded forlornly, each dip of his bobbing head another nail in the coffin, each confirming that until Mrs. Gill had departed there was no real hope of clarifying matters with her parents. Mei-lin's heart sank. She felt as if the ground were opening up and she would plunge into the unending earth and be gone forever.

Dinner was largely a silent affair. The girl said nothing. Her parents, though exchanging a few words with each other, made no real attempt to engage Mrs. Gill in conversation. Anna looked confused and sleepy and mumbled vaguely to herself.

As soon as the old lady retired for the night, Mei-lin joined her. She lay on the floor of the old lady's bedroom, tucked into a musty sleeping bag. The sparse arrangement was less unpleasant than she'd expected. Anna snored softly and evenly, like a kitten purring contentedly, and this comforted Mei-lin. Even so, the awful theory she had developed kept tormenting her. The terrible notion looped and twisted and spiraled in her mind, always evading rationality's grasp, refusing to extinguish itself, checking all attempts at sleep. For the first time in her life, Mei-lin spent the entire night awake, so consumed by fear and dread that sleep was impossible.

$$5$$

Falling Apart

The next morning was a blur of fatigue and confusion. At breakfast, Anna forgot to pour milk on her cereal and, bewildered by
the dry mess of roasted oats and puffed rice in her mouth, spat
her first spoonful back into the bowl. Mrs. Gill, who took only
instant coffee for breakfast, tut-tutted irritably.

"I'm not myself, Fran," said Anna to Mei-lin's mother. "I'll lie
down after breakfast. Cutting down on my blue pill doesn't
agree with me, I think."

"There's not much longer to go. It'll soon be over," said
Fran. "Try not to worry, Anna." Mei-lin's mother went into the
kitchen and started making the girl's lunch. Her father put on
his jacket and went into the garage. They all heard the revving
of his motorcycle as he sped away.

Anna struggled to hold the milk jug. Mei-lin had to pour the
milk for her. Mrs. Gill pursed her lips and, just slightly, rolled
her eyes toward the ceiling.

Anna slammed down her bowl. Fixing Mrs. Gill with a steely
look, the old lady said, "You know, you remind me of someone
I once knew. She had hair just like yours. It was during the war,

in Paris. She spied for the Germans. Everyone knew. In the end, she got shot. Walking home one night, it was dark because of the blackout, someone went up behind her and put a couple of bullets in her brain. Three bullets, actually."

Mrs. Gill gasped.

Anna turned to Mei-lin. "I'm sorry if that story has upset you, dear girl. But that's our history."

Mei-lin shook her head emphatically. She had greatly enjoyed Anna's story. She wondered whether there'd be another very soon.

Mrs. Gill pinched at her blouse, snarling its starchy fabric between her fingers. She inspected her fingernails. Then, recovering herself, the middle-aged woman stood up and glowered at Anna. "I won't dignify that kind of talk with a response, Mrs. Katz. Your kind get away with enough as it is." She turned to Mei-lin. "I'm driving to school in five minutes. Get your lunch, pack your bag. You'll come with me." Mrs. Gill stormed from the dining room.

It turned out that the silver van parked since yesterday outside the house was Mrs. Gill's. Mei-lin sat beside her in grim silence as she drove the hulking vehicle to school. The very second Mrs. Gill parked, Mei-lin leaped out and bolted for her homeroom, tiredness eclipsed by roiling anger.

School was even more dismal than the day before. Mei-lin sat at the back of the math teacher's classroom, filling out new worksheets issued by the principal. Mrs. Gill skulked nearby, a dark, unsettling presence. Mei-lin soon finished the worksheets and, since the library books held no appeal, battled to stay awake as the teacher prattled on about calculus and other incomprehensible things. Whenever she nodded off, Mrs. Gill took a grubby metal ruler and smartly rapped the girl's desk, striking the wooden surface perilously close to Mei-lin's knuckles. The girl pitched into torturous fatigue. Mei-lin felt her head swim giddily. Her eyes became dry as sand; her throat ached; her temples throbbed painfully. Waves of nausea began. Any minute now and, without a doubt, she'd vomit all over her desk.

She worked to slow her breathing. Gently, using both hands, she pressed and rubbed her jaw and neck. Calming a little, Mei-lin gazed outside and her thoughts returned to her theory about Saturday. The more she pondered, the more she examined each crumb of data, the truer her theory seemed. She couldn't understand why they followed the government's orders so readily, without opposition or protest. But that didn't make what was happening any less true. She thought of how terrifying it would be for Anna when they took her to the slaughterhouse. She supposed they'd do it on Saturday morning or, maybe, Friday night. How many others would join Anna there? Would the foreign soldiers be in charge? How would the final coup de grace be delivered?

The girl was overcome by nausea. She fled to the bathroom. Crouching over the toilet, clutching at her long hair to keep it clear of the bowl, she vomited profusely. Once finished, though, her stomach and head felt much better. Staring in the mirror as she wiped her mouth and washed her hands, she suddenly made her decision. She wouldn't go along with the rest of them. She wouldn't keep her head down and shrug off the changing world. No—not at all. She would do what must be done. She would save Anna.

The rest of the school day Mei-lin spent deep in thought. She had little idea how she could help the old lady escape her awful fate. She ran through a series of scenarios: disguising Anna as one of the visitors from up north; hiding Anna in a friend's tree house; smuggling Anna out of town under a tarpaulin in the back of an army truck; finding a hot air balloon and floating away in it; kidnapping the mayor and holding him hostage until he agreed to protect Anna. But none of these seemed more than fantasy. They would work in the children's shows she enjoyed watching on Saturday morning—rich worlds of cartoons, puppets, and camp special effects—but not in the prosaic domain of everyday life.

The day's math lessons ended, Mrs. Gill left the classroom, and the sporting activities of yesterday were repeated. Mei-lin sat cross-legged beside the basketball court. She propped herself up against a squat flight of steps, watching the games listlessly, musing and meditating, turning over the options for saving Anna, marshaling all her intellectual strength to cultivate more ideas for salvation.

The late afternoon sun drooped sedately across the school and the town, illuminating everywhere with its cozy and lovely light. Mei-lin imagined that some supreme force now unveiled them as they really were, stripping all down to the truest soul, a holy prelude to final judgment. She felt on the verge of a tremendous change, passage across some ineffable border between two realms, one lustrous, another foul.

By the time Mei-in arrived home, her mother was just about ready to serve dinner. Mrs. Gill had already positioned herself at the dining table, where she sat with a beady expression reviewing several sheaves of typewritten documents.

"Anna won't take any dinner tonight," said Fran. "She's feeling unwell and she's gone to bed early. The adjustment we had to make to her pills, it's not doing her any good."

The meal was one of Mei-lin's favorites—corned beef

smeared with blazingly hot mustard—and she ate in contemplative silence. Her mind continued to rummage through the options for saving Anna. She had no idea how she'd do it, but she felt sure that Anna would survive Saturday's banquet. Mei-lin's parents watched the girl carefully. Both Fred and Fran seemed somewhat more relaxed, slightly more at ease, as if they were now, at long last, able to observe their child relatively less troubled by the sudden disturbance in all their lives.

As Mei-lin lay on the floor of Anna's room that evening, swaddled in her cozy sleeping bag, the old lady snoring nearby in a slow, regular rhythm, she began once more to ponder all the ways she could save Anna. She returned to an early idea of hers. In the dark, she and Anna would knot together their bedsheets, sling them out the window, climb down like escaping convicts, and slink off and conceal themselves until Saturday was over. She had barely started to picture the old barn they would hide in (the place was clean, roomy, and home to a coal-black mare fond of Mei-lin's shoulder rubs) when the girl fell fast asleep.

6

Heavenward

It was Friday, the final day of the week for workers and scholars, and Mei-lin awoke to the brilliant sweep and pulse of the morning sun, the rays flitting into Anna's bedroom and nuzzling its two recumbent figures like solar angels with shadows made of gold. She got up, had breakfast, and found herself arriving at school in remarkably good spirits. The school day flew by. She finished the principal's worksheets, voraciously read two books she'd brought from home, and keenly ignored Mrs. Gill's presence.

When the bell rang, everyone was dismissed without delay. There were no after-school activities to soak up the day's remnant hours. Instead of walking home, Mei-lin was couriered back to her parents in Mrs. Gill's silver van. On the journey, the two barely spoke. Mei-lin wondered what was greater: her dislike of Mrs. Gill, or Mrs. Gill's hatred of her?

Once they were all home, the Johnsons and Anna and Mrs. Gill sat down and ate an early dinner. These five tense souls slurped bowls of chicken soup resurrected from a paper packet, the bowls paired with plates of dry toast. There was no butter.

The meal was so dreadful that Mei-lin wondered whether her mother had deliberately intended that.

"I know it's not much of a dinner, Mei-lin. But we're in a hurry, I've got so much to do already," explained Fran while they dunked dry bready strips in their thin soup. "There's a big meeting in town tonight. Your father and I and Mrs. Gill will go. Everyone will be there. That is, everyone who's over eighteen but under seventy-five. Mei-lin, you'll stay here with Anna. Get yourself to bed when it's time, don't wait up for us. The meeting will take hours. We won't be back until very late."

Fred began to groan, wordlessly vocalizing his dread of the impending talkfest. Mrs. Gill subdued him with a quick cold stare across the dinner table.

"I think I'll go to bed early," said Anna. "I feel less and less myself. But in the current situation, I suppose it doesn't matter. Time's almost up. Tomorrow's Friday, isn't it?"

"Actually, tomorrow's Saturday," said Fran. "We'll be having the banquet tomorrow."

"Get the thing over and done with, I can't wait!" exclaimed Mei-lin's father, almost spitting the words into his soup. Exasperated, he took up his bowl and spoon and flounced off into the kitchen.

"At least you'll have more room in this house when it's over, Fran," said Anna, regarding Mrs. Gill with calm derision. The old lady lowered her head and, using the loudest possible whisper, said to Mei-lin conspiratorially, "Have I ever told you the story of Eva Braun? Things didn't end well for her, my dear. A lesson for all of us."

Mrs. Gill scowled. Anna tossed her spoon onto the table, stood up, farted audibly, and departed for her bedroom. Her ears ablaze, Mei-lin pitched into a fit of uncontrollable giggling.

The girl had to dash into the kitchen, where Fred had begun washing the dishes. Mei-lin's laughter soon infected her father and he was forced to steady himself against the windowsill as he teetered through a long stint of rebellious, silent guffawing.

Then Fred and Fran and Mrs. Gill all left, setting off in Fran's car for the town meeting. At home there were left only Mei-lin and Anna. The girl knew this was her chance—and probably her only chance. But what, exactly, should she do? She clasped and unclasped her hands, thinking at the speed of light.

She abruptly observed that, there on the floor of the dining room, in its furthest corner behind the dining table's far edge, lay Mrs. Gill's handbag. She mustn't have needed the bag for tonight's meeting, Mei-lin thought. The girl scrambled down and peeked inside. In an instant, she realized what had to be done.

The girl flew upstairs and charged breathlessly into Anna's room. The old lady was kneeling on the floor, inspecting her chamber pot. Anna wore a distracted, absent-minded expression. She'd have to play things carefully, Mei-lin told herself.

"Anna, you know what's going to happen tomorrow, don't you? It's scary. Are you worried?" asked Mei-lin quietly.

"There'll be a banquet. Oh, I've seen worse." The old lady tapped the chamber pot proudly, as if it were a household appliance that had just concluded a difficult household task. "This old thing will come in very handy. I believe the soldiers will come to collect me tomorrow morning. I'm not sure where exactly they'll take us. Perhaps there'll be some nice Canadians? If you want to see the world, French is the language to learn."

A little perplexed, frowning slightly, Mei-lin slipped her hands inside her pockets. "But what they're going to do, Anna …

it's horrible. We can't just do nothing. We have to do something. You know the government people have got the slaughterhouse ready for you, don't you?"

Anna peered quizzically toward a point in space several inches to the left of Mei-lin's forehead. The old lady spoke with a sudden softness, the sentences almost inaudible. "Everything has to happen somewhere. That's what I always say."

Something is off, Mei-lin thought. Something's wrong with Anna. She'd never heard her talk like that before. Her expression, demeanor, bearing … the old lady wasn't herself. For both their sakes, the girl would have to take the initiative.

She went downstairs and rummaged in Mrs. Gill's handbag, plucking away the keys to the woman's silver van. Then she went to the rotary telephone in the hall and jerked the handset up and down. The bell inside jangled each time, an awkward, inelegant approximation of a ringing phone. Mei-lin stood there for a minute or two and went back upstairs.

"Anna, that was my father calling on the phone."

"Really?" said Anna, still kneeling on the floor, her chamber pot now upturned, each hand pressed into its upside-down base as if the old lady were kneading invisible dough. Why Anna had done this, Mei-lin had no idea. "I thought I heard the phone ring," added Anna.

"Yes, Dad says that the car's broken down, they're near the Gibbs's farm, we have to go and pick them up."

"Me? Us? How?" Anna's eyes widened in startlement, large, fearful saucers glistening black and brown and reddish white.

"We will have to go there in Mrs. Gill's van. I've got the keys." Mei-lin dug into her pocket and, flicking out her forearm, flourished the keys showily, the way magicians tug rabbits from hats. "You've still got your driver's license. You said you drove a lot when you were younger."

"Yes, Mei-lin, but I haven't driven in years!" Pulling herself upright, Anna gawped at the keys dangling from the girl's fingers. Their brassy, silvery blades blinked and shimmered in the modest light of summer evening. "I still know how to do it, though. I've driven trucks, tractors, diggers, even a tank once, just for fun. These days your mother takes me anywhere I need to go. Though she's not as careful as she should be in some instances. Dear girl, for goodness sake, don't tell her I said that."

And Anna reached over and grabbed the keys. She pushed past Mei-lin and, as the girl hastened to follow, marched down the stairs and out the door and across the street to Mrs. Gill's silver van. By the time Mei-lin had climbed into the passenger seat, Anna already had the engine going and was adeptly shifting the gear stick. The girl buckled her seatbelt and, after Anna checked in the side-view mirror for traffic, the van pulled out.

Even by the norms of their little town embedded deep in the countryside, the roads were spookily quiet. By the time they reached the town limits, Mei-lin reckoned she hadn't seen a single other vehicle on the road.

"I've no idea where the Gibbs farm is. You'll have to direct me, Mei-lin," said Anna, her hands settled lightly on the steering wheel's upper half, fingers comfortable and secure. "Is it before we get to the roadblock we came across the other night? I don't know whether the soldiers will have gone yet. They might still be there."

Mei-lin thought that the soldiers wouldn't have budged, not even an inch. They'd be guarding all the roads out of town until Saturday's banquet was finished. That's why she picked the Gibbs farm as their target. It was miles before the roadblock.

Though that wasn't the only reason, of course, for choosing the Gibbs farm.

"Don't worry, Anna," said Mei-lin in her steadiest, easiest tone. "I know how to get there."

Up ahead, on the left side of the road, Mei-lin spotted a metal gate. It fronted a dirt lane that carved a relentless unending line through fields of barley and alfalfa and oats, scoring through and through all the way to the foothills. Both her hands gesturing frantically, Mei-lin directed Anna to pull over. The van stopped, and the girl climbed out and swung open the gate. In no time at all, they were bumping down the dirt lane.

"This is the back part of the Gibbs farm. I came here once on a sleepover, we climbed up that tree," said Mei-lin, pointing toward a sprawling beech. "Dad said that they're all up the hill over there. He's trying to fix one of their bulldozers."

"Why does he need our help? Can't the Gibbs people give him a ride if he's having bother with the car?"

"I don't know. Maybe they're busy. Maybe it's an emergency. We can ask him when we get there." To Mei-lin, these lies sounded convincing enough. And there was truth in them: her father sometimes did help local farmers with their broken-down equipment. Anyway, the lying was done for a good cause. Mei-lin didn't feel the slightest guilt.

"Oh, goodness! Who's that behind us?" exclaimed Anna suddenly, staring down into her side-view mirror, blinking wildly.

The girl leaned out the passenger window and, twisting her neck and shoulders like paper that wraps candy, peered back. She had to squint against the dust thrown up by the car's spinning tires. But all she could see were empty fields and empty roads. There was no-one in sight, not a car or truck or motorcycle or anything else that indicated humans in motion. "It's nothing. You're probably just seeing the dust behind us," said the girl. "Don't worry, Anna, we're just helping my father. We're not doing anything wrong."

The silver van reached the foothills and, expertly piloted by Anna, zig-zagged up the dry green face of the sloping hill. Now strewn with gravel, the track cut a jagged line of dusty brown and sickly yellow and sometime gray as it wended upward, ever nearer the sky.

"Look!" cried Mei-lin. "Over there, Anna. See that new road?" The girl pointed to a trail freshly hewn through a rising hillside of grand conifers. "Mr. Gibbs is getting all of these trees cut down. Zach Gibbs is in my class at school, he told us all about it a couple of weeks ago. The forestry company has put new roads in everywhere. They started doing it just this summer." And, thought Mei-lin to herself, there's a real chance the military and government people from up north won't know about those roads. The roads won't be on maps, there won't be soldiers guarding them, no-one will give them a second thought. These new, unexpected roads, little known and easily ignored, would be Anna's route to safety and liberty.

"It looks pretty rough," said Anna, angling head and shoulders forward, scrutinizing the craggy, patchwork surface of the trail cut among the trees. "We'd be better off in a truck. Or even on a tractor. Where do you think we could find someone to lend us one?"

Struggling against sudden rising panic, Mei-lin knew that, to keep the old lady on track, she'd have to extemporize like the best of them. "I think it's fine, Anna," counseled the girl. "My dad's not far up the road. That's what I think. If he could get up there in my mother's car, we can get up there in this van. It's got a bigger engine, and you're a great driver."

Anna lifted her eyebrows, pursed her lips, and puffed briskly. Then, in the fleeting instant it took for that sound to ebb, the old lady's face stilled and firmed. Anna had made up her mind. She slid the van into its lowest gear. Like a huge husk of metal and glass and dirty rubber, the silver vehicle crept ahead, wheels aimed toward the crude trail burrowing through the forest.

Anna and Mei-lin traveled slowly but surely, their path taking them ever higher. Mei-lin knew that, up above, the slope would finally crest and give them a way outward and downward, beyond the ring of mountains that encased their little town, away from the referendum and the soldiers in uniforms and that repurposed slaughterhouse and Saturday's awful banquet. If we can cross over, Mei-lin thought, we can find somewhere safe to park the van, sleep the night away, and then keep ourselves hidden until the banquet is over. The referendum had only happened in her town, Mei-lin believed. Once the two of them had escaped to the outside, there'd be no excuse for those government people to lay a finger on Anna. Mei-lin thought of herself and the old lady living off the land—plucking wild apples, fishing in lakes, sneaking eggs from cobwebbed hen houses—until it was all over and both could go back home.

The trail occasionally developed side branches, lesser tracks snaking away toward left or right, stretching and deepening the reach of the foresters into these woods. Mei-lin commanded Anna to keep on going straight ahead, urging again and again that they'd soon reach her father's position. But when they passed another cluster of side tracks, Anna braked the van suddenly and, issuing a loud groan, flopped down against the steering wheel. Her arms dangled uselessly. The old woman's eyelids clammed themselves shut and twitched and pulsed savagely, as if afflicted by some wicked power.

"Anna!" shouted Mei-lin, grabbing at the old lady's shoulder, pressing and squeezing, shaken to the core by Anna's sudden loss of consciousness. "What's wrong? Wake up!"

Anna groaned again. She lifted her right hand and unsteadily slid it across the dashboard, reaching toward the windshield. Then she opened her mouth, fluttered her lips, and began speaking. "You must promise me something, dear girl." Her voice sounded dreary and older than all the world. "Your father, he voted 'yes' in the referendum. I think he decided the thing was all a silly joke. You know what he's like. And your mother, she didn't vote at all, she thought the whole proceeding was too ridiculous for words. Don't hold it against them, my dear. No-one knew it would turn into this."

Mei-lin's mind went blank. She felt very cold, as if the sun had blinked out, leaving behind only perpetual darkness, all light and natural warmth gone. Why had her parents done that? Why had they been so flippant when they needed to be nothing but serious?

The girl crossed her hands and set them in her lap. Looking down, inspecting her scruffy fingernails, she asked, "And what about you, Anna? Did you vote in the referendum?"

"Of course I did. I voted 'no.' Pity more people didn't do the same." Anna's eyes blinked open and she gazed directly at the girl. "Then we wouldn't be in this pickle, would we?"

"If I'd been allowed to vote, I'd have voted 'no' too," said Mei-lin gruffly, crossing her arms and hugging her midriff. She was shivering, just a little.

Using her right arm to press against the dashboard, Anna levered her body upright. With a clumsy motion of the wrist, she patted the girl on the head, then stamped at the van's pedals and revved the engine until the pumps and pistons shrieked and howled like furious beasts. Moving faster than before, wheels grabbing at the coarse track, they began anew their upward climb.

The sun had almost dipped beneath the horizon when the two fugitives reached the crest of the mountain. Dense rows of pines fell away behind them, stretching down to the foothills, pointing over to the lush fields and dark roads that would, if they so wished, take them back to their little town. And ahead lay freedom and safety: a series of ridges, each lower than the last, stepping down and down toward a long valley split along its middle by a broad, sedate river, grassy pastures hemming the river on both sides, the odd flock of sheep or cluster of sheds and of clunky farm equipment prosaically ornamenting these green reaches. Mei-lin had never been down there, not once in all her life. And so she felt the valley must be remote enough, distant enough from her hometown, to provide sanctuary until the banquet was done and the referendum forgotten about.

"Which way, Mei-lin?" asked Anna, her voice sounding a fearful, confused note. Before them were three separate and independent tracks, each trailing downward: one to the left, one to the right, one directly ahead. Mei-lin supposed that each might take them down to the valley. But she had no idea which track would be quickest or safest or surest. And she could also see, if she craned forward and squinted into the distance, that further down there were tracks leading not vertically to the valley floor but instead going sideways, horizontally, toward other peaks and ridges and foothills, on and on into the hazy distance. Some of those trails, she thought, might even circle around and loop back to the exact place they so desperately must escape.

Anna braked the van. "Which way, Mei-lin?" she asked again. "Goodness, I don't think … Mei-lin, can you …" Her movements clumsy, fingers rigid and unwieldy, Anna knocked the gear stick into neutral, pulled the emergency brake, and closed down the engine. "I need a rest, Mei-lin. Please don't … oh, please don't …" But failing to finish this sentence, drifting off into blankness, Anna slumped backward. She sank immediately into a strange-looking kind of sleep, as if she'd been stopped by time.

Mei-lin gaped at the old lady. Her mind whirred, her eyes narrowed, her lips pursed and tightened. She decided to let the old lady rest for a moment or two. This much excitement probably wasn't doing her any good. Moving quietly, taking care not to wake Anna, Mei-lin turned and pushed open the passenger door. The girl clambered down from the van. She looked about, surveying the three alternative paths before her, the dusty surface of each track, the giant conifers rising above, ample, stout branches swathed in needles of earthy green, then the valley so far below, the range of mountains beyond the valley, and above all this the dome of weak blue sky about to dissolve into dusk and after that detached summery night. There were always mountains, Mei-lin said to herself. In this land, this homeland of hers, wherever you went, no matter how far you'd gone, there was always another chain of peaks and ridges and impossible summits right before you. She imagined a land built by hateful gods who eternally constrained and hindered all those like her.

The girl still couldn't tell which track she and Anna should take. Each weaved and torqued and twisted off through the thick forest much too rapidly for her to figure the actual destination. There was only one thing for it, then. She'd have to get higher, to a point where she'd have a better view. Since they were already on the crest of the mountain, as far up as a person could walk or drive, she'd need to climb one of the nearby trees. A few extra yards of height and she might be able to identify the truest path downward to the valley's floor.

She ran over to what seemed to be the tallest tree. Grasping the broad trunk, the girl hauled herself up, deftly negotiating handholds and footholds around branches and about the tree's coarse bark. She ascended quickly. She felt that she'd probably never climbed one this high.

Mei-lin was about two-thirds of the way to the tree's crown when she paused to survey the scene below. Brushing aside sheaves of pine needles, knocking away a couple of sharp-edged pine cones, she peered down. Yes, she could certainly see more clearly from here. It seemed that the middle track, the one straight ahead of their van, would be best for their escape. That appeared to wiggle down toward the valley floor. But even from this height, she couldn't quite discern the last part of the track, the ending place where it should finally turn her and Anna out into the valley below.

So she climbed higher. For once, Mei-lin appreciated her slight build. The sturdier boys in her grade would have had real trouble now, as the stem and branches of the conifer became thin and slender in these higher reaches. Carefully wrapping her left arm about the trunk, she leaned out to inspect again the middle track as it weaved down the slope.

When Mei-lin swung her body out, though, there appeared something odd and unexpected, an unstable flicker at the edges of her vision. Very high, as high as the best mountains, she glimpsed a sharply metallic thing, swooping through the air and catching the fading light. She turned toward the object, which meant facing the other way, the way they'd come—the direction of her hometown. Even so, against the half-drained sky, thinning and soon ebbing into dusk, she couldn't identify the distant and mysterious thing.

Lower down, though, she caught sight of machines moving, a convoy of steel hulls crawling along the same paved roads that she and Anna had driven to reach the Gibbs farm. To her surprise and shock, she saw the tiny vehicles halt at the entrance to the dirt lane that they'd taken across the Gibbs farm earlier that evening. This same rustic lane had led them onward to the foothills, the beginning of their final journey upward and over the mountain to hoped-for safety and hoped-for liberty.

This couldn't be a coincidence, Mei-lin thought. Someone had seen them huddled inside the silver van, leaving the town, passing fields and farms, coming this way. And so she and Anna had been reported to the government. Or perhaps there was hidden in the van some fantastic gadget, a flashing, squawking device of the kind that spies and secret agents kept handy, and the government clandestinely used this to track the van wherever the clumsy old vehicle went. Whatever. No matter how their absence had been uncovered, how their location had been traced, teams of soldiers and government people now chased close behind, on their trail like brutal hunting dogs.

A thumping, beating roar suddenly charged her ears. From her position in the tree, she made out a black-painted helicopter. It hovered several hundred yards distant, poised ominously mid-air. The dark machine looked as if fixed to a single point in space, a kind of fantastical mechanical hummingbird. Inside she was able to pick out several figures. They were indistinguishable, though, blurry silhouettes with heavy jackets and bulky headgear.

Was Mrs. Gill among them? She imagined the grim dark-haired woman donning a buff helmet, flicking down its shiny visor, reaching with crab-like hands for the flying machine's terrible mounted gun, commanding the crew to get closer and closer. Then Mrs. Gill would lean out the helicopter's gaping doorway and verify with a swift glance that the government's archest enemy, nine-year-old Mei-lin Johnson, had indeed been found, hidden here in these treetops. Grinning like the devil incarnate, Mrs. Gill would pull the trigger and blast Mei-lin to smithereens. Mission accomplished. Roger that. Over and out.

The helicopter drifted closer. Mei-lin still couldn't tell who was inside. She pressed her body against the tree's cragged trunk, burying her face in the crook of her elbow, hoping they would somehow overlook a schoolgirl clinging to the tallest part of an extremely high tree in the middle of nowhere. After a minute or two, the beating sound of spinning rotors softened, reduced, eased. Mei-lin uncovered her face and watched the helicopter dipping away, narrowing into a metallic fleck as it dropped, swooping now toward that same valley where Mei-lin had planned to find safety and refuge for Anna.

There was no time to waste, Mei-lin told herself. She'd have to climb down the tree, wake Anna, and then get the old lady to drive them down the middle track as far as they could before someone intercepted them. They'd probably have to abandon the van and flee into the woods. The odds weren't good. But she had to try, she wouldn't give up. She and Anna weren't going down without a fight.

Swinging her head about, peering between thickets of branches and twigs and cones and sprigs toward the dry, brown, needle-strewn ground, Mei-lin began to descend. She adjusted her small hands by an inch or two; she stretched her feet down the trunk an inch or so. But her torso felt as if it were gummed to the tree, gluing her in place, refusing the option of descent. She'd had this problem before. On an unknown tree, hardly able to see where your limbs go as you clamber down, fear surging like snakes on the attack, the climb back to the ground could be the hardest task of all.

She shuffled and sidled and stole a little further down the tree. Daylight had begun to fade in the rapid, calamitous way it does just before everything—the sky, the mountains, the whirling, gushing countryside of farms and forests—plunges into night. Without the sun, their journey down the mountain to the valley beyond could become perilous. Even with the van's headlamps turned to high beam, Anna would have to drive very slowly, Mei-lin wouldn't be able to navigate properly, and they could miss things essential to their survival. The girl began to feel that time was up, that by now it was all too late.

As she slowly continued her descent, Mei-lin spotted in the distance specks of light clambering up like mechanical ants. They seemed to be climbing the logging track that she and Anna had just ascended. That must be the same convoy of vehicles she'd seen entering the Gibbs farm, Mei-lin told herself. With their pursuers so close, she and the old lady no longer had time to get away down the mountain. Instead, she'd have to coax Anna from the van—hopefully the old lady would wake readily enough from her nap—and the two of them would flee into the trees. There they'd hide out and hope and pray that, huddled low in the dark, the soldiers wouldn't find them.

But Mei-lin had hardly gotten much farther down the tree when the convoy of cars and jeeps and trucks pulled up below, stopping beside the silver van and its slumbering driver. To her startlement, she saw that her mother's car led the convoy. Had the government stolen it from her parents? Or had her mother and father somehow been compelled to join in the chase?

Through the encroach of half-lit dusk, the girl heard doors cracking open and slamming shut, boots thumping against the ground, orders given and responses said, the march and step of men on urgent business, all as if the world itself depended on this. Mei-lin watched a soldier in baggy khaki rush to the van and open the door on the driver's side. Flashlights appeared and grim, pale light washed over the scene, thin as vapor.

"It's the elderly lady, sir. She's unconscious!" came a strained voice from beside the van. "But no sign of the girl."

"Might still be in the tree. Or run off into the forest," spoke another voice. It sounded deeper, slower, older. "Continue the search, men!"

Beams of light flung upward into the treetops. Digging her face into the bark, closing her eyes as hard as she'd ever done, Mei-lin sought desperately to avoid the soldiers' gaze. But her skin pricked and shivered as their flashlights tagged her high position. Even before she peeked down, eyelids trembling and almost closed, she knew that all the people down there had spotted her.

"Sir, she's up there, right near the top of the tree!" cried a voice triumphantly. Several others murmured agreement.

Then Mei-lin heard a commotion break out. Voices were raised, a woman shouted, there were rough, sharp sounds that made her think of jostling and shoving, then an eerie silence, the kind when no-one is able to think of the right thing to say.

From directly below, as if sweeping right up the trunk of the bright-scented tree, sounded the evening's most surprising note. It was the girl's father. "Sweetheart, Mei-lin, it's me. Your dad. Can you hear me?"

Without thinking, answering immediately, Mei-lin called

down the tree that, yes, she could hear him.

"And do you think you can climb down?" Fred asked. "That tree's really tall, and it's gotten dark already."

Then Mei-lin's mother joined the conversation. "It's not safe, Mei-lin. You need to come down now," Fran called out, sounding as if she stood right beside her husband. She uttered something else in a low, percussive, angry tone. Mei-lin couldn't make out the words. They must have been meant for some other person there at the base of the tree.

Suddenly, all Mei-lin wanted to do was climb down, all the way to her parents and the love, affection, protection of each. "I'm trying, Mum. I really am," she cried. "But it's hard. I can only go down really slowly. Like, a little bit at a time."

"Take your time, sweetheart," said her father. "We'll be here all night if we have to. Just get down safely, that's all."

The girl heard her mother barking orders at the soldiers, as if she should've been in charge all along and now was time they knew it. "Spread out, stand yourselves over there, all around the tree," said Fran. "That way, at least one of us can catch her if she falls."

But no matter how much she wanted it, Mei-lin could not make adequate progress back toward the ground. One foot went down, a hand went up; another hand went down, her other foot went up. Time slowed, thickening into sap, advancing barely at all. The world would surely soon stop. Last of all would be her child's body—tiny, minute, dangling far above the rest of them—now almost unreal, now almost gone.

Another voice shrieked from below. "The silly girl's not trying! She's not coming down! She's making fun of us!" Mei-lin's heart froze. It was Mrs. Gill. The enemy stood in their midst.

The girl heard shouting—scuffling and jostling—the sharp scraping of heels against chilled ground. A slight vibration, like the finest arboreal breeze, fled up the trunk and across and through her hands and feet. She peeped downward and saw that, incredibly, Mrs. Gill had started to climb the tree.

The awful woman heaved upward, grunting and croaking and moaning as she climbed. "Get down! Stupid girl!" she screamed. Amid it all, her hair still kept its taut helmut-like shape, scarcely a strand in the wrong place.

Mei-lin thought about pausing her descent or even changing course and scrambling back up the tree. But a strange power, unseen and unnamed, ancient as the turn of seasons, urged her to get as close to the ground as fast she could, off the tree and away from Mrs. Gill. So she continued to scrabble down, her pace quickening, faster and faster.

The trunk shuddered again. There was more shouting from below. Mei-lin's father had started up the tree, climbing hot on the heels of Mrs. Gill. Each moved as fast as the other, her father strong and energetic yet imprecise with his hands and legs, Mrs. Gill older and weaker but galvanized from priggish rectitude.

"Stop!" shouted Mei-lin's mother. "Glenys! Leave our daughter alone!"

"Get away from Mei-lin! Or I'll pull you right off this tree, you cow!" screamed her father, hoisting himself further upward, wincing and spluttering as he grabbed at branches and stamped at crevices and crude spacings in the bark.

Now Mei-lin was only a foot or so from reach of Mrs. Gill. How might she get past her? She contemplated kicking into the woman's hands, at her head, dislodging her somehow. But if she did that, she might lose her own balance and topple from the tree. Anyhow, when push came to shove, when all was said and done, Mei-lin couldn't bring herself to hurt Mrs. Gill. Foul and nasty though the woman might be, Mrs. Gill was still, like Mei-lin and everyone else, human. She thought. She felt. Her heart pumped, her lungs filled, they slackened, she breathed and lived.

Then Mrs. Gill hoisted herself higher. She grasped upward, reaching for Mei-lin's foot. Her knuckles grazed the girl's ankle. Mei-lin jerked her leg away. Her weight shifted to the other leg. But the foot was balanced too weakly across a small bulge in the bark of the trunk, and her grip didn't hold. The heel of Mei-lin's left sneaker slipped away, all purchase lost. She tried to use her arms to save herself, to hug the tree very tightly. But with both legs flying loose, neither lower limb securing any stable perch on the trunk, her hands and shoulders couldn't support the rest of her. The girl's hold failed. She fell from the tree.

Mei-lin tumbled away, down past Mrs. Gill, jolting her knee into the woman's shoulder on the way, apparently dislodging Mrs. Gill too, the enemy joining her in this final fall. They flew down past her father, who gawped in horror at his daughter's plummeting form. The girl dived down, heading toward bare earth, that all lifeless dirt and drifting smudges of scattered pine needles. Mei-lin caught glimpse of her mother, arms outstretched bravely, stumbling toward the inevitable point of impact.

Soldiers shouted. Beams of flashlight heaved, dipped, surged. An angry voice yelled. Boots stomped. Wood cracked.

And then nothing.

7

The Real Truth

"We should think about having you back at school next week. Everyone needs to get on with things." Fran spoke with forced matter-of-factness, the way she commonly did when a thing must be forgotten about and never said aloud again. A sharp breeze pressed into the room, strikingly forceful for this time of day, the still, becalmed lull when breakfast was long over but so many hours yet remained until lunch. Leaning back, Fran scraped the backrest of her chair against the wall and used a single outstretched arm to snap the window shut.

"It's sore, Mum," said Mei-lin. The girl shifted awkwardly in her hospital bed.

"Like the doctor said, your pain medicine was stopped this morning. It might hurt a bit more. Exactly how bad is it, Mei-lin?"

"It's OK, I guess," answered the girl. "I'll see if I can think about something else." She hadn't broken anything when she plummeted out of the tree. Her mother had put herself in the right position in the nick of time; aligning precisely with the girl's line of descent, she'd broken Mei-lin's fall. Still, the girl had been knocked unconscious, and she was bruised badly. The doctors ordered a spell of hospital observation. She'd now spent five nights there in a steel-framed bed, her parents taking turns throughout to sit with her, one or the other always beside her, either Fran or Fred, all night and all day. With one exception—Saturday evening. On Saturday evening, neither could join her, for both had to attend the little town's banquet.

Until this morning, Mei-lin hadn't been able to concentrate on a single specific thing. Her mind drifted, she bobbed and coasted between sleep and groggy wakefulness, she could hardly produce her share of the conversation when the nurses came with food or to check on bruises or help with the girl's toileting. She supposed that painkillers did that to a person's thinking. Now, though, her mind started to settle and fix, to return steadily to its useful natural state. That old question, dormant since she pitched down from the tree, sprang up again.

"What do you think ..." she stammered. "What do you think happened to ..." Mei-lin thought of Anna and what they surely did to her. She imagined the soldiers dragging Anna from the silver van on the mountain's peak, hauling her down to the slaughterhouse, holding her there for the night until the next day's murderous events. She then pictured the soldiers—this now an alternate version of imagined history—gallantly letting Anna slip home from the mountaintop, the old lady glissading through dark streets, wistfully accepting the gift of one last night in her own familiar bed. And the next day a long bus, khaki-tinted and crammed with dry-skinned elderly, came and collected her up and took the lot of them to the slaughterhouse.

With all the other old people, she'd have been installed somewhere in the tidy cottages constructed for abattoir workers, slicers and boners, butchers and packers, knifehands and slaughtermen. One by one, uniformed personnel with clipboards and lawful orders printed in triplicate would direct them through the mechanized halls. The cattle gun would be taken in hand. The bedraggled elderly would line up. The soldiers would stand silent. And at last there'd be done unto these fearful old men and scared old women the same things we do to sheep and cows and swine. Brutal, swift, bloody. And this all attributable to the town's peculiar referendum, those government ministers and lawmakers up north, and somehow also that lady politician, the United States vice president, a blond-haired New Yorker whose tongue curdled its own vowels.

Mei-lin couldn't finish the sentence she'd begun. Surging grief blocked the girl's words. So she nimbly pivoted. "Mum … uh, what do you think happened to Mrs. Gill?"

Eyebrows shooting upward, mouth dropping into a gape, Fran gazed in surprise at her daughter. "Her? I'm not sure, Mei-lin. Last I heard about it, Mrs. Gill was in intensive care. She was injured pretty nastily, she didn't have me to catch you off the tree. A helicopter took her straight up north. Since she wasn't a local, she didn't have to hang around for the banquet." Fran flipped about her forearm and began to pick at invisible lint on her blouse's loose, faded sleeve.

Very deliberately, almost solemnly, Mei-lin's lips formed a question. "So … Mum … uh, what was the banquet like?"

"Saturday? It's over," Fran answered primly. "Done and dusted. Time to move on. Do you know that your dad has fixed the living room window? And my dishwasher's been placed on order. Your dad will have to do some extra hours in the workshop to cover that. Of course, all his own fault."

Mei-lin nodded sagely. She blinked several times. She tried

another angle. "But, Mum, why did everything happen? What was special about that referendum?"

Her mother grew flustered, her cheeks firing red beneath her skin's summer tan. "Um, look, I suppose we can say … it's politics, I suppose. Our little town had its referendum, no-one took it seriously, some people thought it was a complete joke, some just didn't pay it any attention at all. But up north it got latched onto. The prime minister thought we had to come through on our promise. We're that kind of country, he said. He wants to have a national referendum one day soon on our treaty with the Americans. Nuclear weapons, national defense, that kind of thing, it's all tied together. Whatever the result of a vote, we've got to honor it. I think he's getting huge pressure from the American government. Look, it's just politics, Mei-lin. You'll understand when you're older."

Mei-lin thought Fran's answer was madness. She didn't get why things had to be connected like that. How did this excuse what they'd done to Anna? Mei-lin pressed her neck down, forced the back of her skull into the pillow, and glowered at the ceiling. "You know what, I don't want to be a grown-up."

Fran grinned mirthlessly. Mei-lin stayed mute. An awkward silence ensued. Quickly growing tired of her moody glaring at the ceiling, Mei-lin forced her eyes shut and fell asleep. Fran settled more deeply into the chair and idled through a glossy magazine. A nurse brought tea. Then lunch came. After that, hours into the afternoon, a doctor presented himself, looked over Mei-lin, and declared with too much jollity that the girl could be discharged immediately.

"You don't need us here anymore," said the doctor, a pasty, white, clean-shaven fellow in his thirties. He spoke like an old-fashioned English newsreader. "You'll be infinitely more comfortable in your own bed. Any aches or pains, have a go at one of these. They're superb." He pressed a jar of chalky round tablets into Fran's hands. "Just try to put the lot of it behind you, young lady."

During the drive home, Fran stopped at her husband's auto repair workshop. She dashed inside the steel-clad building to tell him their daughter was back from the hospital. Mei-lin waited outside, slumped restlessly in the car. Her father didn't come out. Motoring the rest of the way home, her mother stated that Fred was up to his elbows in grease, halfway through a tricky job, everything very sensitive and his equipment all positioned just so. He couldn't have come out to see his daughter no matter how much he might've wanted to.

They were home. Mei-lin treaded across the threshold and into the compact hall of the house. The hall was the way it'd always been. It was the house's drab center, a bleak and cold no-man's-land. Beige telephone atop basic side table. Wooden staircase treading up to the girl's bedroom and dear old Anna's old room. Opposite the base of those creaky steps, a thin door for passage to the dining room and kitchen and living room, spaces given over entirely to dull practicality.

Standing in the awkward, cold hall, the stifling center of such a parochial home, the girl felt keenly her hometown's small understanding of life's possibilities. Even when she'd spiritedly climbed away, slinging herself up the highest tree on the highest mountain, all in the name of the good and true, Mei-lin had still been pursued like a deadly rebel. Worst of all, when they almost had her, when the bravest might have fought back with a futile last deed, she herself turned. Her only desire was to go down and again become one of them. She'd succumbed like an old sheepdog, lame and trusting, whose master appears one chill morning with shotgun and grave-digging shovel.

Fran had gone into the kitchen and stood by the sink filling the kettle. Approaching carefully, Mei-lin asked, "Mum, can I go inside Anna's room?"

Fran kept silent for a moment, eyeing the tapwater as it flooded into her kettle. Then she answered, quite softly: "Yes, Mei-lin. I'm making a cup of tea. What a good idea."

Scaling the staircase, Mei-lin could feel her heart strain like something consuming itself, shredded to bits and offered up to icy terror. She slowly snuck into the old lady's bedroom. Her small hands trembled, and she stared about wildly, as if petrified of unseen ghouls that might suddenly lurch out from within the room's plain features.

Anna's bed was neatly made, its cotton surface smoothed flat. A wooden chair had been drawn up against the wall. The room's windows were shut. In this early evening of late summer, the sun was honey-hued, its amber beams changing motes of dust into tiny angels. Everything there seemed as it had always been. Except, of course, that Anna was nowhere to be seen. She was entirely absent.

There was something else, too, one other change, which Mei-lin took a few moments to notice. The old lady's chamber pot had gone. Where Anna once kept the polymer container under her bed, now stood only empty space.

From beyond the room she heard the swoosh and surge of fast-flowing water. Though the sluicing, rinsing chords were deeply familiar, their sounds in this context made no sense to Mei-lin. She ignored her ears. Instead, standing with her back to the door, she rested her small hips against the mattress and leaned forward. Propped up on both arms, palms pressing into the duvet for balance, she squinted through the window and out into the empty street, now shadowed more starkly as the sun continued descent.

Beneath, the floorboards trembled. Around, the air stirred. Along her vision's far edges, shadows slunk furtively. Suddenly the girl knew: she was not alone. There was an intruder here, and they'd taken her by surprise. Mei-lin spun about, adrenaline surging, preparing for all eventualities.

Anna paced lightly into the bedroom. "My dear girl, why are you staring out the window like that?" she said, her hands spinning through the air as she spoke, tapwater from the bathroom faucet speckling her knuckles as moist diamonds might ornament ancient parchment. "Are you quite all right?"

Mei-lin's mouth gaped open. Her stomach twisted, her head spun, her knees folded. She slumped backward. Her fall was interrupted by the bed, though, and she flopped down in a half-sitting, half-standing pose. Mei-lin gawped at Anna, the girl's fine-boned jaw levering up and down, entirely soundless, not a single word to say.

"My dear, what's wrong?" asked Anna. She perched beside Mei-lin on the bed and pressed several light fingers against the girl's forehead. "No, you're not hot. No sign of a fever. Although I don't imagine the hospital would have sent you home if you were unwell."

"Anna, I thought you were dead!" cried Mei-lin, her face grave and pale.

Anna took firm hold of the girl's hands and faced her squarely. Eyeing Mei-lin with tenderness, her whole face wrinkling into a broad, wry smile, Anna said: "My dear girl, do I look dead to you?"

Mei-lin shook her head as hard as she could. A sense of deep relief, liberating and marvelous, surged within.

"I must say, I didn't feel overly well last week," added the old lady. "Cutting down on my blue pills wasn't the best idea. Don't suppose there was much choice, though. Thank goodness it's all over. You and I had quite an adventure up that mountain, didn't we? Of course, if I'd have been in full possession of my senses, I wouldn't have allowed it. A very silly idea, the two of us taking off like that. We might very well have been stranded up there forever. But all's well that ends well."

Mei-lin sat goggle-eyed. Blinking stiffly, haltingly, she was quite dumbstruck. She sat and stared at Anna, eyes bulging like a couple of badly poached eggs.

"Made a full recovery, my dear?" asked Anna, tentatively releasing Mei-lin's hands. "No more aches and pains? Falling out of that tree must have been awful. You made a better job of it than that crazy old thing they sent to billet with us. What was her name? Heavens, now I can't remember!"

Mei-lin's mouth again gaped open. "But …" she spluttered. "But … what about the banquet? Last Saturday? So, what happened? The soldiers didn't come and take you and all the old people away?"

Anna smoothed her liver-spotted hands down the front length of her thighs, leveling flat her old skirt's finely plaid fabric. "Well, yes, the soldiers did come. Took us away on a Saturday morning in a couple of buses. Set us up at the slaughterhouse, in the little cottages they keep there for some of the workers. Gave us a lovely lunch. Roast beef sandwiches and lemonade and banana cake."

"But they didn't … they didn't, though …" Mei-lin couldn't get her words out. She shut her eyes and made to breathe deeply, as carefully and broadly as she could, inhaling through her nose, inhaling down to the pit of her lungs, several times round. "So they didn't take you into the slaughterhouse and cut your throat and chop you up and make you into pies or something and eat you all up at the banquet?"

Anna's eyes widened comically, swelling into bright saucers of brown and black and white. Her lips shook, and she voiced a gentle splutter. Mouth puckering and twisting, she seemed barely able to stifle laughter. Her self-control failed outright, and the old lady burst into raucous guffawing.

"Goodness me! Of course not! Obviously no!" Anna slapped her chest with the palm of her right hand, as if to restore emotional poise. "Whatever gave you such peculiar notions, Mei-lin? Did the other children put ideas into your head?"

"No, no! At school we weren't even allowed to talk about the referendum. Or about the banquet, or about anything else like that," answered Mei-lin. "I just thought that that's what was going to happen. I mean, everything was so bad, the soldiers, the town being cut off like that, Mrs. Gill coming to stay with us, like we had to be watched all the time, to stop us getting in their way. I knew it had something to do with the slaughterhouse and all the old people and a big meal, the banquet, which no-one wanted to go to. And no-one wanted to talk about any of this stuff. It just all felt so bad, like people were really going to die."

"You know, you're not entirely mistaken, my girl. There's a nugget of truth in that." Pursing her lips, she twisted about and, facing the dusty window, gazed through its drab glass to the still street outside. "It was bad, we let each other down. The referendum started as a queer joke, you know? Just something for this little town to have a jolly laugh about. People didn't pay the thing serious attention. But once the votes came in, well, instead of just ignoring it, which is what everyone thought would happen, the government up north, the one that runs the whole country, suddenly started hemming and hawing about the result. Things grew very serious when it got linked into international politics. All kinds of theories we heard about a treaty the country was going to sign with the United States, which would be confirmed by a referendum that all of New Zealand had to vote on. The powers that be wanted us to honor our town's little referendum so that the country had no excuse for ignoring any other referendum in future. Set a good precedent, that kind of thing. Utter madness, all of it, if I may say so myself."

Mei-lin still couldn't quite fathom how these revelations fitted together. "But, Anna, why was there that banquet? What was that about?"

"That was the question the town voted on. Whether or not to have the banquet."

"OK." The girl drew in her lips, compressing them between her teeth, suddenly wary of newer thoughts. She paused. After a moment, she said, "But what did you eat at the banquet?"

"I didn't eat anything. The old ones like me didn't go. Everyone else, supposedly it was soup. Thick red soup. That was all."

"Like tomato soup?" asked the girl, mind tumbling in all directions.

"No tomatoes in it, I think. The red color was added, I imagine, to make it somewhat easier to get down. I don't know how they managed to do it, to get it down, but everyone who was supposed to eat a bowl, well, they took what was given them and they ate their bowl of soup. Wanted to get it over and done with, I suppose."

"Anna, I don't understand." Mei-lin frowned severely. She rubbed her right temple with hard resolve, thin fingertips kneading tight circles. "What was the problem with eating soup? What did the soup have to do with the old people?"

"Oh my! You don't know." Anna studied for a moment the space below her bed where the chamber pot sat once. "And now, Mei-lin, I'll have to explain."

As if to allow more room for proper reflection, she edged an inch or two away from Mei-lin and leaned back, using outstretched arms to prop herself up against the surface of the bed. In this position, the old lady told the girl the entire story. Going with the other over-seventy fives to the slaughterhouse. Taking her chamber pot with her, even though this had never been explicitly requested. Carrying out the red-faced demands of officials at the slaughterhouse. Waiting for the army's cooks to stew up red soup in the kitchens there, all kinds of nasty smells wafting thickly through the air. Waiting while the soup was dispatched across town to the residents congregated about banquet tables. Waiting for the vile meal to be sipped, swallowed, digested. Staying overnight in the workers' cottages at the slaughterhouse; journeying home the following day; and then saying as little as possible to Fran or Fred or anyone else about the whole despicable thing.

Mei-lin gasped loudly. Her face whitened. Eyeing Anna fearfully, voice cracking, she pleaded, "Is that true?"

"I'm afraid it is, Mei-lin. That's what happened. They all ate it."

And the girl slammed from the room. She careened into the bathroom. She gripped the bowl of the toilet with loose, clammy hands. As strands of the girl's long and dense hair tossed about her face, Mei-lin vomited repeatedly, again and again and again. She felt she'd never stop. In the end, though, her ragged stomach had nothing left. Like a scorned, betrayed, heartbroken angel, she could only sink to the cool floor and sob in despair.

8

Three Visitors

Years passed. Mei-lin grew up. As soon as she could, she left her mountain-sided hometown. An age elapsed before she thought to return. By then, her own children were almost adults. When she did go again to the little town, it was in the tourist's guise, together with her two sons, eighteen-year-old twins, tall, wide-shouldered, confident boys soon to begin university and make their own way in the world. The three of them traveled all the way from Normandy. The boys had been born there, a moist, gusty, sea-trimmed land long home to Mei-lin and her French husband.

"There's the slaughterhouse," she said as their rental car crawled past the facility, its abattoir still going at full capacity, the cottages for the workers kept in original colors, walls and gardens impeccably bright and tidy, foul stench of burnt flesh also wafting throughout. Mei-lin communicated this to her twins in flawless French, without accent, as if she'd known the language all her life. In the family, they scarcely used English. "This place hasn't changed a bit," she added. "Not a bit."

Her sons knew too well the story of the vile referendum and

their mother's part in that awful affair. But they'd never seen with their own eyes the disaster's mild and pleasant setting.

"There's my classroom," said Mei-lin as they pulled up at the school. The three visitors picked their way across playing fields, concrete pathways, a gravelly basketball court. They boys peered into their mother's childhood classroom. They were alone—being a Saturday, the school was entirely empty. But in her mind's eye, Mei-lin could still see Mrs. Gill sitting at the back of the room, glowering at her plucky nine-year-old frame.

"This place seems pretty normal, Ma," said one of her sons.

"Normal to the point of mundane, I'd say," said the other son, who—though a few minutes younger—had a more fertile way with words.

Mei-lin shrugged. "It was until it wasn't. Who'd have ever thought something like that could happen here?"

"It's hard to believe that the thing all started as a joke," said the older son.

"That's the problem, exactly there," said the younger son. "Laughing off the political process when it's the very last domain we should approach as a laughing matter. Your classic Anglo-Saxon infantilism, not taking things seriously enough."

Mei-lin sighed. "We were just too complacent," she said, stepping between her two boys, the three travelers together treading back to the rental car. "Then it got out of control. Well, you both know the story. And it was only the start. As your grandfather says, the world's been crazy ever since. Maybe even before then. You know what he thinks about Reagan's assassination."

"But doesn't he lodge the blame with female suffrage?" said the younger son, grinning a jaunty, good-natured grin. "Isn't that our original sin?"

Mei-lin swatted her son playfully, left hand lightly cuffing the rear of his head. "Come on, you know your grandfather doesn't mean it." Something in the distance caught her gaze, and she suddenly halted, pulling up her sons alongside, all three stopping side by side. "Over there, if you continue on a kilometer or two, that's where we lived." She nodded toward a line of beech trees that, like lonesome sentinels, bordered the school's playing fields. Beyond, segregated by the row of trees, stood clusters of tidy suburban houses, modest homes for the school's pupils and parents and other denizens of the little town.

Long experience of their mother's wistful storytelling told the children what was next. As one, both sons grimaced in sorry anticipation.

"Imagine what it must have been like for them. The old ones, everyone over seventy-five, including my dear old Anna—may she rest in peace!—marched off to the slaughterhouse. Then defecating into buckets. At least Anna had the good sense to bring her chamber pot, that must have made things somewhat easier." Though her voice kept clear, tears had begun to fill Mei-lin's eyes. From her pocket she drew a small wad of tissue paper.

Mei-lin composed herself, then continued. "After that the cooks somehow collected up all this poop from the old people and they sterilized it. Can you believe that? The slaughterhouse kitchens were set up just right for that, that's why they used them. The sterilized feces went into the red soup. And all the others in town ate it up, these bowls of red soup, quite thick apparently, all cooked with actual feces. At the banquet, they all knew what was in it when they ate it. They were told they had to do it, they voted for it in the referendum, the government was enforcing it, it was compulsory. Get fined, lose your job, lose your house, go to jail if you don't eat it up. So they did it. Totally horrifying."

Still standing between the twin boys, Mei-lin looped her arms about their high, broad shoulders. "I left as soon as I could. Well, it was only a couple of years later than that when your grandparents went as well. You know all that. Emigrating to Australia was what they had to do to get as far as they could from this place. Remember, even though I was laid up in the hospital after I came down out of that tree"—their mother's tree-climbing and tree-falling escapade was famous, eventually reported in newspapers and on television nationwide—"my parents still had to go to the banquet and eat up that regulation bowl of soup made with old people's poop. Everyone had to do it, if they were old enough to vote and weren't yet seventy-five years of age."

The three tourists drifted back across the grassy field to their rented car. Climbing behind the steering wheel, fixing her seatbelt, studying with motherly warmth her older child beside her and her youngest boy in the seat behind, Mei-lin knew again an early truth. This place, pristine settlement in a far land of gentle democracy, was not hers. She renounced it. She would always renounce it.

Just as she'd left before, she left now. She would keep on leaving, always leaving. For as long as her heart could beat, she would leave. As long as her mind could tell right from wrong, she would leave. And she would still leave and leave, always leaving, as long as heart and mind together told her that she and every other person mattered more than all the rest of it.

A Note From The Author

I hope you enjoyed "A Vote For Death." It was a thrill for me to write, especially the twists at the end!

My novel "To Kill A Demon" is—I think—even more thrilling. It's a horror-suspense tale about a young man, Kino Lim, chased by a body-swapping demon. The demon wants Kino's soul, and he'll stop at nothing—extortion, blackmail, assault, kidnap, murder and massacre—until he gets his way.

How can an ordinary man defy all-powerful evil? Well, Kino gets help from some everyday heroes: his amiable roommate, a trigger-happy female cop, a headstrong rideshare driver, one no-nonsense cleaning lady, and a mysterious blind woman from the future. Will they all be enough, though, to defeat the devil?

To find out what happens in "To Kill A Demon" (especially its jaw-dropping finale!), you can go online to edwinbrightwater.com/getbook2. Or you can use your phone to scan the QR code here:

To give you a taste of "To Kill A Demon," I've also included the first chapter after this note.

Happy reading!

Warm regards,

Edwin Brightwater

PS If you haven't already joined my mailing list, I'd love to have you. I'll only email you when I have news, and I'll never share your details with anyone else. To subscribe, please go to my home page at edwinbrightwater.com.

First Chapter Of "To Kill A Demon": A High Balcony, Before Christmas

Onto the high tower's highest balcony trod three ill-fated men. The old priest came first, then the priest's young lover, and, trailing those two by a few feet, a tall, fat banker in a three-piece suit. As they crossed the balcony, none knew that one of these men would shortly be dead. But his murderer—treacherous, cold-blooded, evil—was already there.

"The view is superb, isn't it, Ravi?" said the banker to the priest's lover. "This is one of the finest penthouses in the country. Not the biggest, certainly, but one of the loveliest. I expect you haven't been about many places like this, Ravi. Have you?"

Ravi grinned shyly and shook his head. He did not speak. Though beautiful (long eyelashes, skin rich and dark, lips and chin and cheekbones of a prince), Ravi was barely out of his teens.

The priest moved to his lover's flank, the two men standing side by side at the balustrade, shoulders almost—but not quite—touching. They looked out over the city-state's old harbor and new finance district (so prim, so smug) as if they were captain and first mate of a proud ship, its mission vital, its cargo precious, the two seagoers assuredly eyeing things over as the vessel readies to set out.

"My goodness," said the priest. "This is all fresh pastures for young Ravi. We old folk will have to go gently on him." The priest was more than twice, much closer to three times, Ravi's age. He was slight, especially about his shoulders, and tended to stoop. Though many men of his race (southern Chinese whose forebears huddled down to the equator before air-conditioning and today's antimalarials) were this way, it was still unexpected in one so successful. For the priest had done very well by selling God to a soulless land.

Ravi grinned again. He turned from the view over their tiny country (it covered less ground than New York City; to drive across took less than an hour) and found the priest's gaze. Ravi blinked; his eyes sparkled like diamonds flung into the sky.

The priest stared and gaped, enamored, enraptured, ensnared. He stood perfectly still, immobile, as if the poison of a sly viper had set in. Then his face clouded, his head dropped, and he drifted backward, away from Ravi, away from the balustrade and its view, toward the wall of glass doors and glass windows slashing down the balcony, a glistening threshold between the wide world out here and the boxy cavern, pastel and airtight, that was the penthouse's living room.

His wife stood there—in the living room, there on the glass wall's other side—soaked in the rattling din of a cocktail party, a colorless drink in one hand, the other extended with its palm downward, like a soldier marching forward. She was slightly younger than the priest; she stood even shorter. Smiling joyfully, the priest's wife seemed to be showing a cooing clutch of guests something on her wrist

The wife and the other partygoers kept together on their side of the glass, crowding into the living room where the air was deliciously chilled. Though late in the afternoon and just a week before Christmas (in strict terms, it should have been the start of winter), things were as they mostly were on this tropical island: far too hot—almost ninety degrees—to be comfortably outside. In the living room, amid the party, no one took notice of the balcony; there the three men could be quite alone.

As the priest peered through the glass at his wife, a hangdog look, coiling furrows of shame and regret, crossed the old man's face. Sinking lower and lower, tottering, failing, he grabbed with one hand at the balustrade.

This was it. The fat banker would seize his chance. "We need something to drink, Ravi. Kindly track down a couple of beers for Pastor Frank and myself. Nothing local, thank you. You can do that, can't you, Ravi?" said the banker. He glared at Ravi; the lover flinched.

"My young ladies will prepare anything you ask," added the banker. "The smoothies they make are positively world famous." He jerked his head in the direction of the seven young women, a troop of pale-skinned northern Europeans, who, through the glass, could be seen threading among the guests, bearing platters of drink and food, their seven faces all oddly blank, as though drained of something essential.

"They take a few minutes at least, even if it's just one smoothie," said the banker. "People serve under me, they've got to do things properly. But we've got time. Pastor Frank and I can wait for you. Ravi? Ravi?" Impatient already, the banker again twitched toward the partygoers in the living room, his shudder urging Ravi inside, as if Ravi were a sheepdog working a flock of sheep.

Ravi slid open a heavy glass door and went in. The banker went and stood beside the priest. Now it was just the two of them, two rich men whispering into the wind.

"Now, tell me, Frank," demanded the banker. "You and that queer-looking boy. What happened?"

"It's the Devil. The Devil did it, Sam. The red beast, he's got to me again," said the priest, his brow furrowing. "It's impossible, Sam, there's no way out. Not this time, it's gone too far." Hardly anyone called the banker by his first name. But Frank and Sam went back a long way.

"Very well. What happened, Frank?" said Sam again, his tone searching and urgent. He drew himself high, towering over Frank (Sam was tall as well as fat), and tugged at the lapels of his linen jacket. He was lavishly overdressed for the tropical heat.

Even so, Sam did not sweat; his coppery skin shone dully under the sun's rays, as if it were an infernal mirror that repelled every fleck of unwanted light and still never returned any image. For Sam was different from Ravi and Frank. His ancestors came not from India or China but from hot places much closer to this prissy island and from cooler realms much further away: the Malay Peninsula, on the maternal side, and the dead empires of Europe—Holland, England, Portugal—on the male side.

Frank sighed loudly, restarting his hard-working engines of self-pity, girding himself to reply to his benefactor. "You know what I've been through," said Frank. "You know the trauma I've had, it's been almost twelve months now, but it's not getting easier. Sam, I can still see her body. I know she was a slut, but …" He stopped and sighed again. "Look, I had to have an outlet, somewhere I could just be me. Ravi's in a line of business where he can help with that. A little pick-me-up, letting off steam, he has the stuff for that. Just pills, of course. Well, sometimes powders as well, you take a snort or two, the world changes."

Sam glowered like a cloud so black, so despondent and hateful, that it'd destroy the sun with its very first peal of anger. "I see. Ravi's a drug-dealer. Just as well, then, that you have the Attorney-General for a brother-in-law. We should thank the heavens for all of your connections. You're going to need them." Testy, frustrated, using his meaty left palm like a bludgeon, Sam batted the balustrade's uppermost rail. His eyes narrowed. "But Ravi's not just a drug-dealer, is he? He's a whore, too."

Frank recoiled in horror. "No! Not at all! It's nothing like that."

"He does it for free, does he, Frank?" Sam looked disgusted.

"Of course, the drugs, yes, I pay for those, naturally, that's what you … yes, well, it's …" said Frank, his sentence spiraling away into wordlessness. He looked over to the city's downtown skyscrapers, as if something there might marshal his response. Sam waited coolly. One or two seconds of stiff delay went by; then Frank turned to face the banker again. "We started taking the stuff together. He doesn't normally do that with clients. But he did it for me. I opened up to him, I shared a lot of my history with him, it was very intimate. We started holding hands, cuddling each other. I've never had that kind of intimacy, not with anyone, certainly not with either of the wives. Pretty soon it became … well … more intimate. Things got sexual. Not just sexual, though, almost spiritual, really, more than sex, yes, much more than sex. It was intense, so intense, unbelievably intense. We were seeing each other every day. That's when I hired him as my chauffeur, had him coming to church, sitting there in the front row, I wanted people to see that this was a young man I was trying to help, a lost soul I was introducing to Christ."

Sam was horrified. "Frank! Frank!" he spat. "Didn't you look at him? Didn't you see him?" Roughly, with the back of his hand, Sam wiped his lips, cleaning away excess spit. "Couldn't you tell how black his skin is, Frank? Turn off the light and, poof, you wouldn't know where he was. You'd have to put a bell round his neck. I bet the grinning pickaninny hasn't graduated high school, probably still mouths the words when he reads." Anger contorting his large face, Sam shook his head bitterly. "You're a pastor, for goodness sake. Cavorting like that, abusing yourself, violating the order of nature—sick, just sick! And with an Indian mouth-breather besides, as if you couldn't find one of your own kind. What were you thinking? Frank? Huh?"

Frank began to cry. Tears ran lightly down his cheeks; he blinked madly, snorting, whimpering, blubbing; his chin puckered. "Oh, please. I know. It's the Devil, he's forced me, he's made me do it. All the good work I do, sharing God's love, that's the reason, that's why. The darkness hates light. Of course, choosing Ravi, using someone like him, Satan knows where I'm at my weakest. He's as crafty as he's evil. Lost souls, I'm drawn to them, I'm driven to share with them God's grace. But this time, Sam, the Devil got to Ravi, got to him before I could."

"You're right, Frank," said Sam. "Satanic forces are at work—certainly. They've taken over that mincing little curry muncher. Degenerates, perverts, sickos like him, their souls are born twisted. He's already corrupted, rotten through and through, all the way. He came out that way. What's happened, what the Devil's done, it's inevitable." Pursing his lips, Sam gazed directly, fixedly at the priest. "Now, tell me, Frank. Look me in the eye and tell me. What would you have me do to help?"

Frank sobbed louder, air harshly jerking from his lungs, ragged wheezes and gasps of self-pity. "Yes! Please, please! I need you, Sam. I need you to help me, more than ever. I always thought that what happened last time, with the girl, was bad. But this is worse. It's much worse." Frank looked up, imploring, desperate, into the red sky of late afternoon. "Lord, please, what have I done to deserve this?"

Sam waved at Frank impatiently, the fingers of his right hand jolting through the air like fretful butterflies, spasmodic and dismissive. "Calm down, Frank. The girl was different. That was a major problem! True, usually no one cares much about missing housemaids, least of all the glassy-eyed Indonesian variety. I give you that. But she was pregnant—thanks to you—and some goody-two-shoes pathologist might have decided it wasn't the sleeping pills that finished her off. Who knows, perhaps a couple of feathers from the pillow got stuck in her windpipe? Worst case scenario, an investigation starts and your idiot brother-in-law can't get it closed down. Then it'd be over for you, the church, all of us. Everything we've built destroyed, all our good work wasted. That's what I'd consider a disaster." Sam frowned dourly and, as if to punctuate this dark expression, twisted his head from side to side and gruffly tut-tutted.

Then his frown faded and he began to smile. "But we got lucky. I had my camera. Hiding the body was a cinch. And now," said Sam, his smile wider and brighter, "they all think she scuttled back to Indonesia with your wife's jewelry. This time, though"—the smile was fading—"if we have to get rid of a body, I won't be able to use my camera, Frank. It's no longer in my possession. I've lent it to a colleague. Sorry."

Frank went goggle-eyed. "A body? The camera?" he cried. "No, no! Not to Ravi. I couldn't stomach that. Sam, we're in love. We love each other!"

"Two men? In love?" said Sam, grimacing sourly, rolling his

eyes. "You sicken me, Frank. But don't fret. I know where the line must be drawn. What about your side of the bargain, eh? Do you have any leads on that other matter? I need my sustenance, remember." His eyes flickered over to the living room on the glass wall's opposing side, where Sam's guests still picked at food and drink delivered up by young, smooth-skinned, slightly sullen European women. "Those ladies, their tour of duty is almost over. Time for a fresh cycle."

"Oh!" replied Frank, taken aback by the conversation's sudden turn. "Yes, actually, I do have something, well, someone—I should say—in mind." From his trouser pocket, the priest produced a cell phone. He prodded the screen and gawkily flipped the device around, offering it to Sam like a student submitting an essay late. The fat banker took the phone with both hands. "That's him," said Frank, wagging bony fingers at the image on the screen. "That's the one."

Pursing his lips, Sam squinted at the image. "Mmm. Name?"

"He goes by Kino."

"Looks like he's Chinese," said Sam, leaning down, getting closer. "Kino's not a Chinese name, though, is it?"

"No, not at all, no. Kino is his first name, his Christian name. He's Chinese, though, the family name is Lim."

"Ah," said Sam. "Lim. Trailer trash, I expect. What's his story?"

"Young Kino joined our flock at the start of the year. The poor boy was lost—truly, truly lost. I personally took him under my wing, showed him the way to the Lord. Now he's one of our most reliable members. He's a true inspiration, just the kind of young man religion was built for." The priest paused, coughing modestly. "What you asked for, Sam, was someone who's still struggling, who's constantly being tested. I'm sorry to say this, but Kino's like that. He wants to come to the light, to be pure and holy, but he's constantly tempted by sin, he can't shake it off. In my opinion, he's always going to want the church. And, naturally, we'll always be there for him."

Sam smacked his lips. "Delightful! What a treat! This boy could be the answer to all our prayers. Can't have me running out of steam, can we? What a morsel. Now, Frank, when is this Kino Lim available? It's got to be sooner rather than later. Otherwise no point wasting our time with him."

"Uh … look, in fact, he's currently abroad, he headed overseas to brush up his Mandarin, says that might help with his job. But he's planning to—actually, I believe he's confirmed to, it's locked in—come back before Easter. You'll be able to take him then."

"Easter?" exclaimed Sam. "You're pushing it. You're really pushing it. I suppose, though, if I apply myself, work hard to conserve my energies, I could wait it out. But no longer than Easter, Frank. After that, it's a total no-can-do. Absolutely not." Sam shook his head briskly, like a dog shaking water from sodden fur, as if the very act finished the issue. "Now, my friend. Do tell me. Where's Kino Lim studying? Beijing, is it? And what's his line of business?"

Frank answered these questions in a quiet, even, modest tone, as though he knew the answers would provoke Sam but there was, in the end, no way around it.

"Ugh!" spluttered Sam. "Disgusting place. And Mandarin's useless for a low-end salaryman like that. No wonder the boy's all lost. Kino doesn't know what he wants. Hah—whatever it is, he can't have it! Really, though, what makes him so delicious is—and this is the nub of it—he doesn't know who he is. Now you've shown him to me, of course, he's never going to find out." Sam carefully drew the phone and its image of Kino Lim close to his coppery face, near enough, in fact, that a moderate extension of the tongue would have had him licking the screen. "He's perfect for me."

Frank smiled proudly, his shoulders lifting, his face smoothing, eyes squarely meeting Sam's gaze.

"Let's seal the deal," said Sam. Gripping the phone with his left hand, Sam reached out with the other; Frank placidly slid his own hand across Sam's; the two hands clasped and, in the usual way of their desiccated, self-centered clique, the men made their agreement. Whether a trick of the afternoon's dying light or some other power, it was hard to say; but, as Sam released his grip, his coppery, leathery, hard-worn skin somehow emanated a dark, bloody red.

The glass door that connected the balcony to the living room heaved open. Ravi appeared in the doorway and, delicately clutching two slim-necked bottles of beer, stepped onto the balcony. Squalls of frigid air and banal music—festive, upbeat, born-again—tumbled out through the open door. Acting quickly, blushing like some embarrassed schoolboy, Ravi pushed it closed. The air stilled. The lonely balcony was, once more, quiet.

Passing the beers to Frank and Sam, Ravi said that his smoothie (mango with special Russian ice cream) was still being made up. But it was hot outside and he thought the two men on the balcony, who even though so busy and so important had still been very kind to him, shouldn't be left to wait for their cold drinks.

Frank smiled warmly and thanked his lover, the young man's guileless ease soothing the old priest's guilt and shame. Sam absentmindedly tapped the neck of his bottle, frowning into the distance, glancing with furrowed brow over the balustrade, where almost a thousand feet below tiny cars drove along tiny roads and tiny humans, almost unseeable with the naked eye, stepped along tiny paths.

"Ah!" said Sam, his face unclouding, speaking to no one in particular. "Quid pro quo. It's time." He handed his bottle (he hadn't had a single sip) to Frank and, as if the thing were a drum, pounded the balustrade with his open hand. "Ravi! Come and look. Enjoy the view. Enjoy it!"

Ravi laid his fingers across the chrome railing and craned forward. Looking downward, his face sank until its profile became horizontal, the invisible line that slanted from his nose down to his chin now parallel with the earth. In a light tone of polite amazement, he said that so far down everything looked really small.

And now Sam was ready to return Frank's favor. He stepped away from the balustrade, planted his feet leadenly, and, hands by his sides, clenched his fists tight enough to make the knuckles turn the color of ash and bone, milky sick and deathly faint. He grunted over and over, each time louder and harsher and sadder. On his last grunt, so loud and sharp that it was just about a shriek, Frank and Ravi both swung around, turning to him, the priest and his lover now perturbed, unnerved, almost alarmed.

The world was silent. From the other side of the balcony, where the wall of glass doors and glass windows held back the living room and its babbling party, came no sound. From below, from the streets and parks and office buildings of the city, it all lay still and soundless. Even the wind, occasionally ruffling treetops and flags and freshly washed clothes at this time of day, had receded into void silence.

"Look!" cried Sam. "The birds, Ravi. See the birds!" He

pointed toward a small flock of starlings. Suspended in the air a few hundred feet from the high balcony, the birds were motionless. Their wings did not beat; their claws and beaks did not draw up or strike down; their lungs and throats gave no sound. It was as if, mid-flight, by force of magic, time had been frozen and, the laws of physics no longer any concern, some devilish power had left the starlings hanging in the air, hopelessly stuck.

"The party, Ravi. What about the party?" asked Sam, spinning around and pointing to the living room inside its wall of glass. The guests, the waitstaff, everyone within, stood frozen in place, rigid and lifeless like shop floor mannequins or broken-down automatons.

Mouth gaping, slack-jawed and goggle-eyed, Ravi gawked at the scene behind the glass. He looked over to the birds suspended mid-air; then back again to the frozen partygoers; and once more to the birds. Awed and horror-struck, Frank threw his hands to his face and retreated away from Sam and Ravi.

"What do you think, Ravi?" asked Sam. "Eh?"

Though Ravi's lips twitched and fluttered, he spoke no words. The magic trick had left him speechless.

"This is my power, Ravi," said Sam. "This is it. You might say, I suppose, that I have a special—indeed, an extraordinary—connection with time. Stop time here, freeze time there, pull us outside the flow of time for a serious conversation, I can do all of that, Ravi. Right now, for the three of us, standing here on this balcony, the whole world has stopped." Sam waved dismissively toward the furthest corner of the balcony. "See that security camera? Even the electricity powering its circuits, even that has stopped, Ravi. Incredible, don't you think?"

Ravi nodded grimly. He looked over at Frank, whose head had flopped down, face cradled helplessly between thin hands, eyes fixed uselessly on the balcony's tiled floor. Ravi opened his mouth, as if to ask something, and then turned back to Sam. "Are you …?" he stammered. "Are you … God?"

"My boy," said Sam, "if I were God, I wouldn't tell you, would I?" He smiled as if he were a doting uncle just arrived with a trove of Christmas gifts. "Look again, Ravi. Down below. What do you see?"

Ravi leaned over the balustrade for the second time that afternoon, peering down at the tiny cars and tiny people below, his slim frame edging further outward and further downward. Now his hands—smooth, fine, beautiful—barely touched the railing.

"Uh," said Ravi, "I can't really see anything very clearly, we're too high up, everything's so small down there."

"Mmm," said Sam. "Then, my boy, why don't you get a bit closer?"

In the blink of an eye, in a fluid, single movement, Sam stepped toward Ravi, gripped the young man's collar with one hand and his belt with the other, heaved him up into the air, and, as if the banker were throwing out a bundle of old shirts, tossed Ravi over the balustrade. As the priest's young lover fell to his death, plummeting a thousand feet or so to the asphalt street below, he did not scream or shriek; there were no yelps or whimpers; there was only astonished silence.

Frank cried out and dropped down to his knees, his old, thin hands trembling, kneading and smoothing his face, its surface now bone-white and stretched taut as parchment. Bemused, Sam dusted himself off (though his clothes were still somehow starkly clean) and went to Frank. As the banker drew the old priest upright, sound and movement returned to the world. The starlings restarted their flight; again the wind blew lightly; once more could be heard the sounds of the party and seen, through the glass wall, guests speaking and drinking and smiling.

"What's wrong with you, Frank?" said Sam. "This is what you wanted. It's certainly—oh yes, most certainly—what you needed. A young homosexual jumping to his death, taking his own life just before Christmas, when you were trying your level best to minister to him, to steer a sad lost soul toward the Lord, it's terribly unfortunate. But these things happen. And we're all better off without him. You know that, Frank. You've had your fun. Time to move on."

Frank wiped away his tears and peeped up at Sam, unsure, hesitant, weak as all those men who worship the wrong gods. "Will it seem like a suicide? Really?" inquired Frank. "I suppose … if the camera was stopped, if everything was frozen the way you usually do it, Sam, if no one in there at the party could see what was happening, well … I suppose …" With Sam supporting him by the elbows, Frank dabbed with a handkerchief at his own nose. "But Sam … what does … how do I …?"

Grasping Sam's forearm, the priest began to move away from the balustrade. The two men made their way side by side toward the glass wall. Frank looked straight ahead. "We'll need to call an ambulance," he said. "And the police too. But Ravi's family, I think it's best that I tell them myself, in person. In this business, the personal touch is everything."

They were almost at the door, several guests already staring out through the glass—they squinted, they frowned, they could tell something had happened—when Frank stopped suddenly. "Sam, I don't know. I can't say," he said, still looking ahead, into the living room and its cocktail party. "What do you think?

Why is this? Why is it?" Holding his breath, Frank spotted his wife; she looked at him fixedly; he blinked and looked away. The priest sighed. "Sam, can you tell me," he said, mumbling, almost inaudible, "who am I?"

Pained, caustic, Sam rolled his eyes. "Pfft! None of that matters," he said. "Just do what you're supposed to."

And the two men went inside.

To read the rest of "To Kill A Demon," please go online to edwin-brightwater.com/getbook2. Or use your phone to scan the following QR code: